FOREWORD

This book could not have been written without the help of the following people to whom I owe a great deal of thanks.

My wife Hazel, for your patience, understanding and love.
My boys, Conor and Calum, my reasons for getting up in the morning.
John, for the continuous consultation and for providing me with the mindfulness needed not only to complete this but to help with my fight against Parkinsons.
Marc, for being the other half of Marks, as well as always being there.

AUTHOR

Steve Fyffe is a former police officer who was diagnosed with Parkinson's disease in February 2012.

He continued to work as a police officer albeit in a modified role in the Family Protection Unit for approximately four years before he retired from the police due to his deteriorating health.

He began writing as a form of therapy for his increasing anxiety which is one of the many symptoms of Parkinson's.

Chapter 1

Conor Marks is a 26 year veteran of the police during which time he has had spells in CID, drugs branch, intelligence unit and of course in uniform. Most of his service had been spent in CID in Dundee, during the late 80's and throughout the 90's when murders in Dundee were common for a city of this size. He has risen from constable to Chief Inspector in CID. However, any hopes of progressing further up the ladder were well and truly smashed about a year ago he was diagnosed with Parkinson's disease.

Since his diagnosis, his life has changed dramatically. He has had to become more selfish and put himself first which sounds easy to do, but when you've lived your life putting other people well-being before your own, it goes against your nature. But now he has to consider several things before he sets out to complete a task. Even the simplest task can be quite taxing, and he must consider different things depending on the day he's having. On a good day, he can do what he has always been able to do, it just might take him a bit longer.

However, he has to remember that his capabilities can change very quickly such is the unpredictability of Parkinson's. Therefore he must ask himself, not only can he complete the task, both physically and mentally, but if the task going to take some time to carry out, will he retain his focus for that length of time. Can he physically complete the job without it wiping him out for the rest of the day? There is a long line of questions he must ask himself before he does anything, that a healthy person wouldn't even think about. Will I be able to write this report before my writing becomes unreadable? Will my hands work long enough to type a report? Will I manage to walk the quarter mile from A to B, and even if I can I need assistance at the end of my journey if I need to go to the bathroom?

The list is endless. One person Marks met at a Parkinson's group meeting recently summed it up perfectly.

You're at Tesco's. There are 3 checkouts open, all have queues, what line do you go in? A healthy person would say the shortest one. But what if the shortest queue requires you to pack your own bag, which also has to be done quickly, or there is a display which will have to be avoided/walked around. The Parkinson's sufferer may be having a bad day and not have a great deal of dexterity in their hands and so will say whatever one allows me to get the checkout operator to pack my bags. They may be unsteady on their feet and so opt for the queue where they don't have to negotiate walking around something.

On the rare occasions when Marks would be in a negative frame of mind, he tried to reassure himself that at least he could count on the love and support of Susan, his ex-physiotherapist. He always wondered how people who lived alone coped.

Susan understood Marks' need to take his medication at set times, and the effect Parkinson's has on him. She knows if he is having a bad day and how best to support him. She'd moved in with him a few months ago, although it wasn't a conscious decision made by either of them, she stayed a few days one week, a few more the next, until she had practically moved in. It was the next step in their growing relationship. Not that Marks would have had it any other way. He was very happy. In a strange sort of way, Marks had Parkinson's to thank for Susan.

He found himself enjoying having his dinner at a regular time, of course it helped that Susan was an excellent cook. He enjoyed watching tv in the evening with Susan on occasions, although he preferred to read a good book, Steve Fyffe being his favourite author. He wasn't a fan of soap operas, but he did like watching crime dramas. If he was being honest with himself, he was enjoying the whole experience of having some structure to his day. He'd worked shifts for years, changing shifts at the drop of a hat. He never seemed to have the same routine for too long. For the first time in his life he had a feeling he was part of a family outside of the police. Every milestone in his life had been celebrated either with his police colleagues or on his own. Now he spent his time with Susan and her relatives he was seeing that there was more to life than police work. He wouldn't change a thing from his past but if he had developed a relationship with someone when he was younger, he doubted he would have reached the rank of Chief Inspector.

Initially he struggled working Monday to Friday office hours. He hadn't worked office hours for years. Although it did make taking his medication a lot easier than if he did shift work. There were tablets he had to take every four hours to assist with his movement. One for depression, that comes with Parkinson's. One for his stomach to protect it from the Parkinson's medication. He also had tablets to take if he felt he needed an immediate boost. He quickly found out that the medication must be taken at the same time every day, because that's when the body will be looking for it.

Thankfully, his system was now used to the tablets. For some reason, best known to the doctors, he wasn't prescribed anti-sickness tablets when he was first given his Parkinson's medication. The week he started the medication he was constantly sick, every day for a week. He couldn't keep anything down, not even water. By the end of the week he felt as if he had done a thousand sit-ups. He'd never experienced abdominal pain like it.

He found that he had to eat smaller portions more often than the usual big meals at lunch and dinner. When he did eat a big meal, he really struggled for energy. But he was warned not to eat a protein packed meal 45 minutes either side of his medication because the consultant neurologist informed him, that the human body will always take the protein from a food-based source before it takes it from any other source, like the medication.

Since his Parkinson's diagnosis Marks had adapted the way he approached life and work.
He had to listen to his body, if he felt tired then gone were the days of surviving on coffee and adrenaline, he would rest. At times this meant sitting down for half an hour whilst he regained some energy. He was becoming aware of his limitations too.

Although he could still do most of what he was able to do before his diagnosis, the recovery time from doing these things was sometimes three or four times as long. He could no longer stand for lengthy periods of time, walk up-stairs without getting out of breath or even write for too long before his writing became illegible.

People think Parkinson's is all about the person shaking. Marks was no different and thought the same. But as he was finding out, there was a lot more to it than that. Parkinson's is a collection of symptoms, thought to be about sixty of them, but there were that many that everyone had any number of these symptoms. This was one of the biggest frustrations for Marks.

One day he could have 6 symptoms, the next 10 – and they could be a different symptom from the previous days. There was no logical pattern to it, and he struggled to understand things that could not be explained logically.

Marks felt extremely frustrated at times, especially when he wanted to do a simple task that ordinarily would take him a matter of seconds but could (on some occasions) take him 10 – 15 minutes. Like going to the bathroom, putting on a pair of socks and shoes, getting dressed, having breakfast or lunch. Anything that required dexterity now caused him a problem, that included things such as, tying shoelaces, buttoning up a shirt or even undoing zips, all tasks that seem so simple yet can cause such frustration in a Parkinson's sufferer.

The unpredictability of Parkinson's, was also, in Marks' opinion, the main reason there has been no cure yet. What affects one person may not affect another and for there to be a cure, they (research scientists) would have to find a way to stop the brain cells that produce Dopamine from dying off. Then they would have to find a way to get the dead brain cells to work again. Either that or find a way to replace the dead brain cells with new stem cells. However, that itself is very difficult to do because the stem cells would have to be manipulated to become dopamine producing cells. Current research into this, is in Marks' opinion is the best hope we have of finding a cure not only for Parkinson's but for other diseases too.

Marks continued researching about Parkinson's.

Stem cells research is not new a new concept. But the rate in which researchers are consistently learning about how to develop stem cells for their particular benefit (each researcher will have his or her own goal – to cures for diseases, early detection of diseases, regeneration of organs, body parts etc) is nothing short of astounding. This filled him with hope. Although he was positive most of the time, there were days where he found it tougher to cope with things.

Parkinson's sufferers work better when they have a routine according to all the websites he had looked on. Marks' knew that and he tried from day one to have good routine. His morning routine would start at 6am, (Even at the weekend). He would do a 10 minute stretching routine, have a shower, eat some breakfast, drive to work, have a coffee whilst the computer was firing up, have a bit of banter with the night shift DO's (Detective officers) and then get down to work.

Work would start with him checking to see what crimes had occurred during the last 24 hours. Picking up on the more serious crimes and making sure they were highlighted for the attention of the early shift.

There was a lot less stress in his life now. The settled home life helped.

Despite not being on operational duties, he was still involved in the investigations into major crimes, mainly as an interview advisor. This allowed him to use his innate talent to untangle the lies the suspect would spin and uncover the truth. Although he rarely carried out interviews now, he still frequently advised detectives on what questions to ask suspects based on the evidence at hand.

MONDAY

It was early on Monday morning, and DCI Marks was sitting in his office. The door was closed. Marks was enjoying the silence before the mayhem began. He took a mouthful of his first coffee of the day. It may have been decaf but it was brilliant. It was the only way to start a Monday morning. He sat there, enjoying the silence, broken only by the smooth efficient whirrings of his computer as it loaded the necessary programs for the day.

He looked around his office whilst he savoured his coffee. There wasn't much in his office. It was small and quite dull really. Although he had a small window the view was of another part of the building. At least he could see it was a day when you'd rather be outside than in. A sunny morning with the faintest of breezes, the perfect morning for a stroll along the esplanade. He looked at the walls of his office, one wall had a photo of a much younger Marks at police college alongside some much younger looking colleagues, most of whose names he could still recall. On the wall behind his desk was the much-prized photo of him shaking hands with the legend that is Jim McLean, the much-revered ex-manager of Dundee United. He had taken Dundee United from a corner shop team to a supermarket of a team known throughout Europe in the 1980's. A feat that will long live in the memory of everyone at Dundee United.

On another wall a calendar, with various meetings written on in pen in numerous days throughout the month. Whilst on the wall above his computer were files and a few law books. They'd always been in his office, although he couldn't recall the last time, he looked at them. Then again, he knew what was required of him in any investigation such was his experience. He took the last gulp of his coffee almost at the same time his computer system sprang into life.

He gave a little sigh, as if he were getting tired, but he didn't even know himself if it was due to how he was feeling today, or in general with work. Here we go again he thought, before he plunged himself deep into the world of crime. He began reading the incidents that had occurred over the weekend. Carefully noting the more serious crimes and looking at how they had been investigated so far. Despite his wealth of experience he maintained his level of compassion for the local street bobby, who had acted with good intentions upon their arrival at the scenes of crimes, only to unintentionally destroy evidence. Unlike some of senior colleagues who were only too pleased to verbally batter the uniformed cops at every opportunity, Marks liked to educate them so they wouldn't make the same mistake twice. Although he was quite pleased with the standard of uniformed officers work. There was and would always be mistakes made, especially by those eager to make a good impression, some of them being too quick to show how clever they were that they made a basic mistake.

He knew most cops were hard-working and enthusiastic. Of course, there are always some, as there are in any line of work, who are lazy, some who are just not cut out for police work, and some who wouldn't think twice about dropping someone else in the shit if it meant covering their own arse. He wasted no time in bringing them to task.

He was almost up to speed on things when there was a knock at his door.

'Come in'.
'DCI Marks?'
'Yes, how can I help you?'
'Hi, I'm Calum Sharpe, the new Detective Chief Inspector of CID.'
Marks had almost forgotten that there was a new DCI starting today. Marks felt like this was another stepping stone to get rid of the old and bring in the new. He was getting replaced by another DCI whilst his old partner in crime DI John Thompson had been promoted to Chief Inspector but as a result of this, had to return to uniform to obtain the promotion,

which he felt was a shame because Thompson showed real promise as a senior detective.

Marks saw that Sharpe lived up to his name, at least in physical experience, and how he presented himself. Sharp suit, crisp white shirt, gold tie, black well-polished shoes you could see your face in, and gold cufflinks. Anyone would be excused if they thought he was going to a wedding. Marks had heard through the grapevine that he was very clever too. Won the academic award at college, had a degree in Psychology and had common sense too. A very useful trait to have, although Marks could name several cops who sadly lacked in this area, but that didn't make them bad cops.

'Good morning, I'm DCI Conor Marks. Pleased to meet you Calum', I didn't think you'd be here so soon'
'Thanks sir. Traffic wasn't as bad as I thought it would be'
'Please call me Conor'.
'Ok.'
'Good. Have you met any of the team yet?'
'No I wanted to meet you first, seen as it's your job I'll be doing'.
'Ok. Well let's grab you a coffee and I'll introduce to the team'
Marks had known the man for about forty seconds but was very impressed already.
'Sounds good. How are you feeling about being taken off the investigative teams?'
Marks thought it was abrupt question to ask being that they'd just met, but he liked the no nonsense talk. He was too long in the tooth for idle chit chat, which quite frankly bored him.
'It's unfortunate because I enjoyed doing what I was doing, but I guess I shouldn't complain because I've been in CID for nearly twenty years, been part of some great enquiries and worked with some great cops.'
'You worked on the golf course murders, didn't you? That must have been horrific to see but interesting to work on'.
'Yeah. You're right on both accounts.
'Wasn't the killer an old friend of yours?'
'Yeah, how did you know that?'

'They speak about it at police college, on the DI training courses. How you dealt with the whole incident. It's regarded as one of the best investigations carried out'.

'I just did what I had to do'.

Sharpe got the impression that Marks was uncomfortable with the adulation and changed the subject.

'I'm looking forward to working in Dundee. It's one of the cities I've never worked. Is there a lot of major crime here?'

'Not compared to Glasgow or Edinburgh but I'm sure there will be enough to keep you busy'.

'In here' said Marks as he led Sharpe to the kitchen. 'What do you take in your coffee?'

'Milk one sugar'

Marks made the coffee and handed it to Sharpe.

'Right, we'll go and see the detectives'

They entered the CID office. It was a large office with many desks and computers, much like any other CID office, with the odd plant thrown in for decorative purposes. Another sign Marks was getting old was the absence of cigarette smoke hovering in the air like sea fog. Nowadays fewer people smoked, he's sure he had seen an air purifier beside someone's desk too. Although it was quiet now as soon as the office fills up it can be a noisy, busy office.

It was 0645am and there were only a handful of detectives in the office. They were the night shift CID. They fortunately weren't called upon too often as they were only available for major incidents, such as rapes, robberies and murders. The early shift would be in any minute now.

Although early shift CID were due to start at 0730 hours, they often came in about half an hour early to bring themselves up to speed about what's been happening. Parking was a nightmare at headquarters. In true Police Scotland style, their best ideas in saving money was to relocate various other departments to headquarters. What they did not take into consideration, however, was that there was the same number of parking spaces as there was 20 years ago when there were fewer cars and staff working from HQ. This meant that staff came in late from time to time thanks to not being able to find a parking space near the office. There is a multi-storey car park opposite headquarters, but it is very expensive to park there.

Marks saw that two of the Detective Sergeants were already in the sergeant's office.
Lisa, Jimmy, there's somebody I'd like you to meet, 'this is Calum Sharpe, your new DCI'.

'Morning sir' said Lisa smiling as she stretched out her hand to shake Sharpe's hand. He smiled back at her and shook her hand. You didn't have to be a detective of any note to see the instant attraction between them. Then again, Lisa Bailey, was a young intelligent, very attractive woman and Sharpe, well, Marks had never gave it a thought before about how good looking another man was but he could tell that being 6ft plus, muscular, with a full head of well-groomed hair, nice smile and a glint in his eye, that Sharpe was no stranger to the ladies.

'Morning sir' said DS Budd, who was a young, fresh faced lad, with light brown hair, designer glasses, sharp suits and ties. He was a good guy, an enthusiastic, happy go lucky guy that everyone liked.

'Good morning sergeant' said Sharpe as he shook his hand.
Bailey quickly informed Marks that she would be happy to introduce Sharpe to the early shift. Marks said with a wry smile, 'that would be great Lisa, thanks but I'd like to bring DCI Sharpe up to speed before I give this morning's briefing'.

'Oh okay' said DS Bailey, clearly disappointed.

Sharpe gave Bailey a smile then followed Marks to his office.

Marks explained that there is a third DS that works in the department DS Jackie Gold but that she was on holiday for the next week, then would return on late shift next Monday. She was a very keen officer and was the most experienced cop in CID, (with the exception of DCI Marks) having been in the department for 15 years.

Chapter 2

FRIDAY

It had been a relatively quiet week for CID in Dundee, which suited Sharpe because it gave him time to observe his staff, review their workloads, see how they interact with each other and find out what each of his detectives' strengths and weaknesses were. He was pleased to have found that all his staff were hard working and they all seemed to work well with one another. This was unusual. He had found in every other office he worked that there was always two or three people who didn't get on. But he hadn't seen any evidence of that in Dundee.

Late Friday afternoon and they were getting prepared for another busy weekend when there was a knock at the door. Tony went to see who was at the door whilst Martin continued making up the deals in bags of £10 and £20. It was a little earlier than they normally started dealing on a Friday, and they weren't expecting anyone but Tony opened the door anyway, and as he did so he was smashed in the face. The blow sent his backwards. He tried to look up, but his eyes were streaming with tears from the excruciating pain in his now bloodied face. He'd been punched before but never like this. As he lay on his back the last thing, he saw was a large boot stamping on his face.

When Tony came round, he couldn't feel anything in his face, it was completely numb. His head was throbbing, his breathing laboured. He picked himself up and wiped the blood from his face with his hands, he could taste the blood. *'What the fuck just happened?'* he thought as he stumbled into the living room. 'Martin, Martin you alright?' At first, he couldn't see Martin, he looked round and saw him lying in the doorway between the living room and kitchen. Motionless, Tony's immediate thought was that he's dead. He checked for a pulse, but he couldn't find one. Doing his best not to panic, he dialled 999. He tried to tell the emergency operator what the problem was, but because of either his thick Scouse accent or broken nose, or combination of both, she struggled to understand him. He ended up shouting for an ambulance and said his mate was dying which fortunately she understood. He looked at Martin and could see his forehead had a clear print of a large boot on it. His face was covered in blood and his nose and cheekbones were clearly broken. He put Martin in the recovery position then waited for the ambulance.

Tony looked over to the table. Shit! Where's the fucking money? Where's the gear? They'd been robbed. But he couldn't phone the police. What would he say to them? Yes officer there was approximately ten grand in money, a kilo of Cocaine, about fifty bags of Heroin and a small quantity of ecstasy, that's all they took. He would have to explain this to his boss. He was gonna be fuming. Tony could hear him now shouting something like 'Somebody had the balls to rip us off. Well I'm gonna castrate the bastards'! Someone would pay for this. Tony sat beside Martin, talking to him, trying to bring him around. All he could think about was how pissed off his boss would be and who is stupid enough to rob a Liverpudlian drug dealer?

The paramedics arrived a few minutes later. Martin's pulse was weak. Tony couldn't recall what he said to them or what they said to him. That was the last thing he could remember.

Meanwhile in Aberdeen, Robbie drove down another street he was unfamiliar with. They'd found the right street at last. Bloody sat nav. More bother than they're worth.

It looked just like any other house in an area of Aberdeen that was unknown to Robbie and Sean. A semi-detached 2/3 bedroomed house with a small side garden leading to the rear of the property which was fenced off. On the side gate there was beware of the dog sign which had clearly put up to ensure none of the neighbourly children went in the back garden to retrieve their ball. Robbie was sure that unlike some people who put these signs up to deter burglars, the occupant of this house probably had at least two Rottweilers called Tyson and Killer which would gladly take a bite of your arse should it find itself in their garden.

There was a small front garden with the lawn cut short. It was split by the small path situated down the centre of the property which led to a front door. The door was made of pvc which generally came with a five-lever lock system. Sean knew that doors of pvc construction although lighter than wooden doors, are harder to force open. Sean knew this because he had been in a few houses throughout the years that have raided by the police. On one occasion he was in a mate's house, when police battered the door down. He'd been asleep on the settee, having spent the night there at a party. He'd had too much to drink and fell asleep on the settee. He was awoken however by the crashing sound of the police smashing in the front door. They'd battered the door with such force that the entire door was battered off of its hinges and before anyone could do anything the police were in the process of slapping handcuffs on them.

However, when he had been at Chantelle Court's house some months ago, police attempted to raid the property. But because Chantelle had a pvc door, which was locked at the time, the police took ages trying to get in. They made such a noise trying to batter the door open, that everyone in the street had time to look out their windows and see what was going on. The police destroyed the door, but still needed Chantelle to let them in. If there had been drugs in the house when the police started to batter the door down there definitely wouldn't have been any drugs by the time, they got in.

Robbie parked up in a side street where they could watch the house without making it to obvious. They watched the door because they had a lot riding on this and had never been to this house before. This was Sean's biggest deal and he didn't want anything to ruin it. Nearly half an hour they had watched this door and nothing. No one had come to the door or left from the property. Robbie and Sean were starting to think they were wasting their time when a car pulled up to the house. It was a brand-new Jaguar F-Pace. Must be £50,000 worth of car there thought Robbie.

They eagerly watched to see what happened next. They couldn't see inside the car due to the tinted windows. They were extremely keen to see who Mr Big was, but instead they got to see his right-hand man, at least that's who they thought they were looking at. He was at least 6ft 6 and was a musclebound giant of a man. Robbie could see why he would be someone's right hand man, their enforcer. It would take a brave man to argue with this guy. He looked around menacingly, to see who was watching. Thankfully, he never noticed Robbie or Sean, who by this time had lowered themselves into their seats just enough that they could see what was going on.

Robbie and Sean were thankful they weren't seen because they didn't fancy explaining why they were watching the house to the big guy. He didn't look like the kind of guy that would appreciate someone sticking their nose into his business.

This big guy calmly walked to the door of the house. Someone was clearly watching because the guy was only halfway to the door when it opened. This was the dogs' cue to start barking, although Robbie thought it was more like a roar. He momentarily drifted into a daydream, whereby he was envisaging two Jehovah's Witnesses walking up the path, only to hear those roars, followed by the Jehovah Witnesses turning and sprinting out of the garden to the safety of the street. Robbie smiled.

The door opened and a small, bald, rough looking male answered the door. Nothing was said between the pair. The big guy handed over the holdall and took possession of the rucksack handed to him by the smaller male. The bald bruiser closed the door whilst the tall male got back in the Jag and drove off. There was no screeching of tyres or wheel spinning nothing dramatic at all.

Robbie and Sean remained in the car. They had been told to be at the address at 6pm. However, Sean was paranoid. Maybe it was this paranoia that kept him ahead of the police. He only trusted a few close people, and Robbie Beaumont was one of them.

They had about twenty minutes to wait.

Robbie had become Sean's driver and right-hand man over the last year, of course this meant he had become more involved in the drugs scene, which for Robbie had been a far easier thing to do than he ever thought. Once upon a time he loathed drugs and everything that came with it, but now it was making him a wealthy man. He had soon realised that he could make more money in a night selling drugs than he ever could working as a labourer on building sites. However, this was one of the reasons he rarely spoke to his brother, Barry, who was a police officer, but not the main reason, that would be his gambling, which had already caused a rift between them.

At exactly 6pm Sean received a text from an unknown number stating their parcel was in stock and free to be picked up whenever they were ready.

Sean got out the car and started walking over to the house. He was constantly looking around him, after all he was in an area he didn't know. This meant he wouldn't know any of the people in the street, who for all he knows they could be undercover cops. At least in Dundee he knew a few of the guys in the drug squad. He didn't know who he was looking out for but hopefully he would know if he saw it. But all he saw was four kids playing football further up the street, a few more younger kids playing on a trampoline in a front garden and two elderly males talking to an elderly woman in her garden. No one appeared interested in Sean Murray or what he was doing, which suited him fine. He opened the gate and walked up the seven steps to the path, his heart was racing and he was trying to tell himself to calm down, he didn't want to give this guy any indication he was nervous or inexperienced at doing this. He also wasn't too fond of dogs, especially giant man-eating dogs that sounded like lions. As cool as he was playing it, if one of those dogs got out and was as big and fierce as it sounded, not only would he run like Usain Bolt, but likely, he would shit himself! As he approached the door, it opened.

The bald male who had previously answered to the giant about half an hour earlier was standing there. He looked even rougher up closely, not the kind of guy you would want to piss off. He reminded Sean of the wrestler 'stone cold' Steve Austin.

He didn't look that small anymore, Sean thought he was probably about 5'10-5'11, bald with squashed nose which looked like it had seen its fair share of punches. He wore a t-shirt that looked too tight for him, although Sean thought it's because of the size of the guy's muscles that are making the t-shirt look tight. It would probably be baggy on me.

Sean looked at the guy. The guy looked at him, as if he had done a shite on his new shag pile living room carpet.

'Yeah, what'd you want' said the hardy guy.
'I'm here to pick up a package' said Sean confidently.
'You got something for me'
'Yeah, here' said Sean as he handed the guy a rucksack.
'Wait here' said the male as he took the rucksack and closed the door.
Sean thought *what the fuck am I gonna do if he doesn't appear with the gear. If he doesn't come out. I'm gonna must knock on this door and ask where my money is. That could hurt.*
But he needn't have worried because within a minute the guy re-appeared with a different rucksack and handed it to Sean.
'I'll be in touch' said the guy before closing the door leaving him standing there looking into the bag.
'Thanks' said Sean. Although he had never carried out a deal of this size before he knew not to look inside the bag until he got in the car. He was buzzing. He hadn't even noticed but Robbie had turned the car around and driven up to the gate. He got in the car and Robbie drove off.

'Well' said Robbie.
'Give iz a fuckin chance' said Sean as he looked in the bag.
A big smile appeared on his face.
'Superb. We're gonna make a packet this weekend alrite' said Sean excitedly.
Robbie smiled 'what? Do you think we'll sell the lot over the weekend?'
'Yeah, no worries. I've got a guy that's recently moved up from London who's wanting a quarter of the stuff himself, apparently he has contacts in the clubs that will sell this shit no problem'.
'Yeah, sweet'

'The rest we'll sell no problem. I've been battered with texts and calls all week from people that have been given my number from mates'.

'How do you know they're not cops?' asked Robbie.

'Robbie, c'mon. You should know by now; I've got friends in the right places' Sean said with a smile on his face.

Robbie smiled and nodded his head, 'cool'. But he was thinking I wonder if he knows Barry's a cop.

But Sean never said anything, and Robbie didn't feel like sharing this.

Robbie focused on driving whilst Sean started texting and making calls. Robbie could hear the quantities of weight people wanted and the prices they were having to pay. From what he was hearing Sean was selling thousands of pounds worth of gear and they weren't even halfway home. That night was unbelievable. Not only did they party hard, but they were rolling in money.

SATURDAY

The next morning, Tony awoke to several nurses scurrying about tending to patients. His head was agony. After a few minutes he managed to get the attention of one of the nurses.

'Good morning. How are you feeling?'

'My head's aching. Where am I?' said Tony. He knew he was in hospital but didn't know which one and what ward he was in.

'You're ward 15 in Ninewells hospital in Dundee. The paramedics brought you and your friend in yesterday. Do you want something for the pain?'

'Please'.

'Ok, just be a minute' said the nurse as she walked away to get him something for his headache.

She returned a minute later with some Ibuprofen. 'Here take these' as she hands him two tablets.

'Thanks' he put them in his mouth, at least he thought he did but it was hard to say because his face was so sore and swollen'.

She gave him a drink of water. He managed to take enough of it to help wash down the tablets although most of it went down his t-shirt.

'Nurse. What happened to the guy that came in with me?'
'I don't know. I'll find out and let you know' she said, before she turned and walked away.
Then he fell back asleep.

When he woke up later he was told by a different nurse that Karen, (the nurse he spoke to earlier) had asked her to tell him that his friend was stable in intensive care.

Tony thanked her for passing that on. For a brief moment his mind drifted from his own aches and pains but they soon returned. He lay there wondering how his life would have panned out if he'd completed his apprenticeship as an electrician, one things for sure he wouldn't have ended up here today.

Chapter 3

SUNDAY/MONDAY

Marks was at home when his mobile phone rang. It was Dave Black, a good friend of his who was also his line manager. Unfortunately however, it was not a social call but one of a serious nature involving a serving police officer.

Black had received a call from Tom Kelly, a Detective Chief Inspector with the Scottish Crime and Drug Enforcement Agency. Barry Beaumont, whom Marks had met on several occasions at social functions but never in a professional capacity, had for the last year been working undercover. He was trying to infiltrate a drugs gang that were thought responsible for flooding the area with extremely potent batches of Cocaine and Heroin.

Black knew that drugs gangs that are trying to establish themselves in new areas often introduce stronger than normal batches of Cocaine and Heroin, because this gets people hooked very quickly on the drugs. After the drug user has tried the stronger of the drugs, they find that their next bag of drugs they get from their regular dealer isn't strong enough. But they need to get another hit and the only way of doing this is, is by buying the drugs from the dealers that have provided them with the higher potency drugs. But of course they find that the gang have reduced the strength which leaves them needing to buy more bags to equal their last hit. But now the person becomes more desperate for the stronger drugs. Now they're hooked and desperate. Needing to fund their habit they then turn to crime. It's a vicious circle and unfortunately, it's one that most drugs users find themselves in.

Dundee officers were keen to stop them in their tracks for these reasons and they didn't want any more youngsters getting hooked on drugs. Nor did they want this notorious gang, renowned for being extremely violent towards anyone who had crossed them, getting a stranglehold in the city. Barry Beaumont had been handpicked by Tom Kelly because of his previous police experience in the drugs branch.

As part of his duties he had to call Kelly or text him a safe word, every three days to ensure he was safe. The call didn't need to be long, just long enough for Kelly to recognise it was Beaumont on the phone and for him to say he was safe.

Black was the only officer out with the SCDEA (Scottish Crime and Drug Enforcement Agency) that knew about Beaumont's role.

It was 9am, Sunday morning, and Louise had awoken to the sounds of birds singing and the sun shining but she noticed that Barry hadn't been home again. Over the last few months Barry had begun staying out overnight more frequently. However, he had assured her it was necessary for his work. Nothing else was said. She knew not to ask, not that Barry would tell her anyway, but she didn't want to put him in an awkward situation. She trusted Barry, always had, at least until he'd cheated on her. But she would put this down to a one off incident and he had never given her cause to think he was with another woman again. Then again that's been three nights he's been away for and she hadn't heard from him. This was very unusual even for Barry.

She phoned his mobile. It rang out. She text him asking him to let her know he was alright. She wondered where he could be although she tried not to think of what he could be up to because the thought of something happening to him was not worth thinking about. Despite the brief affair he had, he was still the love of her life.

Louise made herself a coffee with her new coffee machine Barry had bought her for her birthday, whilst she was going to relax by reading the Sunday papers. Louise remembered Barry saying he would be out of town for a few days, but he never said where he was going or with who.

Louise hadn't even begun to read the papers; she was just sitting in the kitchen enjoying her coffee when there was a knock at the front door. She jumped. The knock clearly startled her.
Louise looked at the kitchen clock 09:27. She wasn't expecting anyone.

It was DCI Marks. Whilst he didn't usually work Sundays, due to the nature of this investigation he had no choice but to come in to work. Marks and Louise had met on several occasions at social functions and had always got on well. Louise liked Marks' honesty and quick wit. Louise obviously looked shocked at Marks' presence at her door on a Sunday morning.

'I'm sorry if I startled you Louise. Can I come in?'
'Yes, of course' said a shocked Louise. 'This way' said Louise as she led Marks into the conservatory, via the hallway and kitchen.
'Please have a seat. What can I do for you today Conor?'

Marks sensed she was wanting to know as soon as possible the reason for his visit. This was fine by him because he wasn't one for idle chit chat.

'It's Barry'

As soon as he said this, he could see panic etched on her face.

'I'm sure it's nothing to worry about, but we need to know where he is' said Marks quickly.

'Barry?'

'Yes'

'My Barry'

'Yes'

'I don't know. I haven't seen him since Thursday evening when he said he was going away for a few days. I never asked where he was going because he said it was work related but that he expected to be home today. Why?'

'I don't know if Barry's told you what he's working on. Unfortunately, I can't say what it is. All I can say is we have reason to believe he might be in danger.'

'Barry. I'm sorry Conor there must be some mistake Barry usually works in an office from Headquarters. I know he must go to the Police college every so often which means he has to stay away overnight, but he's rarely gone for more than 2 nights at a time. At least that's what he's told me'.

'And you believe him?'

'He's never given me a reason to not believe him.' She kept his previous indiscretion to herself.

Well, he does work from Headquarters from time to time, but he works undercover, so often he's not in an office. I'm sure he never told you so that you wouldn't worry. But it's imperative we speak to him as soon as possible' stated Marks.

'What do you mean he could be in danger, from whom? What's he involved in?' asked Louise who was by this time was getting very worried.

'Barry has been working under cover for a number of months now and because of this he has to check in with the office every couple of days.

'Every couple of days. What the hell is he doing and what makes you believe he is in danger?'

'We've received information that the people he is investigating may have found out that he's a police officer. Although we can't be sure if they have found out his real identity, we can't take the chance and we need to get him out of the situation as soon as possible. That's why we need to know where he is' said Marks

'Of course. I can't believe he never told me' said a dismayed Louise.

'Like I said. He obviously wanted to protect you, that's why I'm guessing he never told you. Do you know where he is?'

'No, I don't. Like I said I didn't ask, but then again I don't generally ask when it comes to Barry's work'.

'Does Barry have more than one mobile phone?'

'Not that I'm aware of?'

'Can I just check his mobile number ends in 2693?'

Louise quickly checked her phone for Barry's number 'Yeah that's his latest one'

'Do you know what he was wearing or what he packed to take with him?'

'Jeans, a shirt and he'll have been wearing his black jacket. But I'm not sure what he would have taken with him.'

'Does he have bank cards with him?'

'Of course'

'Has he mentioned anybody he works with or keeps company with?'

'No. He never speak about his work'

'Ok. Well thanks for your help Louise if we find out any more information, we'll give you a call. In the meantime if you hear from him can you let us know?'

'Of course'

'Thanks'.

Marks tried to reassure her all would be fine, but deep down he knew if the people Barry was investigating had found out he was a cop, then Barry would be living on borrowed time.

Marks knew they had to act fast.

He returned immediately to headquarters. On entering the CID offices he nodded to Sharpe indicating he wanted to speak to him. Sharpe broke off the conversation he was having with one of the Detective Constables and walked to Marks' office where he met Marks.

'We've got a problem. I want you to come to DS Black's office. There's something we need to discuss' said Marks. Sharpe never said anything he simply gave Marks a little nod of the head indicating he understood.

Marks knocked on the door of the Detective Superintendent's office.

'Come in' said Black.
'Morning Dave'
'Morning Conor, Calum'
'Have you filled Calum in on what's happening?'
'No I just got back from speaking to Louise and I came straight up here'
'Ok. Calum this is what's happened so far. Barry Beaumont, a detective sergeant in the Scottish Crime and Drug Enforcement Agency has been working undercover for almost a year infiltrating a drugs gang from Liverpool who have flooded Dundee with high strength batches of Cocaine and Heroin. He's been building up a file on who the main players are, and things were coming along great. However as part of his duties, he's to check in every three days via a phone call or text to say he's alright. But he hasn't phoned and hasn't text the safe word. Granted it's only been five days since he last checked in, but he's never missed a check in. We've also received information from an informant that the gang know his real identity. Obviously if this is the case, we need to get him out NOW. This gang are known for their brutality towards their enemies.'
'How confident are we that the information from the informant is genuine' asked Sharpe.
'We can't afford to not treat it as genuine. What did Louise say?' Said Black.
'Unfortunately, she had no idea Barry was working undercover. She last saw him on Thursday evening, but he never speaks about his work with Louise. She did say however, that he expected to be home on Sunday'.
'Well let's hope he turns up today'
'Calum just one more thing. This stays between us. It's only us that know about Barry's current role'.
'No problem'
'We'll see if he returns home today if he hasn't returned by 6pm then we'll see about pinging (getting a signal from) his phone and see what we

get from that. Conor, I want you to identify a two DC's that we can trust to keep this to themselves in case we need to take things to the next level'.

'Will do'

'Keep me updated'

At that Marks and Sharpe left Black's office.

It had just gone 4pm when Marks dialled Beaumont's home phone number. Louise answered. He knew Black had said they would start looking for Beaumont if they hadn't heard from him by 6pm, but Marks couldn't wait that long. He asked Louise if she had heard from Barry, but she hadn't. She was understandably worried. Marks tried to allay her fears but felt Louise Beaumont was an intelligent woman who knew the trouble Barry may be in. He didn't want to treat her as if she were stupid and say everything would be fine. All he could do is tell her he would give every effort to try and trace Barry safely. She appreciated Marks' comments, but unless Marks traces him safe and well he will feel like he has failed, not only Barry but Louise too.

Mark put the phone down and decided to initiate a missing person investigation, but he would be sure to mark it as a confidential document. This would allow him to permit access to the report to a chosen few people. This would allow the investigating officers to carry out enquiries secretly.

Marks called Sharpe to let him know what he was doing and that he would like him to task two detective constables to investigate Beaumont's disappearance. But he would need to select two DC's that could carry out diligent enquiries without rousing suspicion from anyone. He would need to divulge Beaumont's alias to them and so it was essential that they kept what they were doing from their colleagues. In order to do this Marks thought it best that he allows them to work from a separate office.

Marks got started straight away on the paperwork required to allow them to try and pinpoint where Barry Beaumont's mobile had been used. This is done by triangulating a signal from a number of phone masts which will then give an indication as to where the phone is now, by accurately calculating the time the signal takes to bounce from a phone mast back to the phone. Once it has done this from two or three phone masts it will pinpoint the phone down to a few hundred metres. Marks knew this is a major tool in the police's toolkit when it comes to tracing missing persons. However, this information could be hours old, so Marks was hopeful Beaumont would have used his phone recently.

Meanwhile, Sharpe had dedicated two officers to carry out this enquiry. DC's Angela Sharma and Mike Munro who were to coordinate their efforts with Marks.

Marks had listed several tasks to be done but trusted Sharma and Munro to prioritise them whilst he pushed through the mobile phone location enquiry via the appropriate channels. This would take a little time, but this would then allow Marks to carry out enquiries with Beaumont's bank. He was hopeful it would show that he withdrew money from an ATM which had cctv.

Marks discovered that the licensing office wasn't being used today, so he arranged for Sharma and Munro to work from there for the time being.

Chapter 4

TUESDAY

Marks awoke at his normal time 0530 hrs. He hadn't slept particularly well. He couldn't put his finger on it, but something was bothering him about Beaumont's disappearance. The neurologist did say he'd have good days and bad days and that there would be no pattern to this. The experts couldn't be any more accurate because there were simply too many unquantifiable factors to consider. Today was going to be tougher than normal. He woke up feeling tired. When this happened in the past, he found himself struggling more than he normally would. But he couldn't let tiredness ruin his day because as time went on, he would find himself having more days like this. It was something he had to overcome occasionally.

He arrived at Police Headquarters slightly later than normal. He said his usual hellos to the staff at the public enquiry office and to Ann the cleaner, who cleaned the CID offices. He noticed that his office door was open. He wondered why it was open because even the cleaner doesn't go in his office when he's not there. On reaching the door he noticed his computer was on and all the programs required for him to carry out his daily duties were up and running. He saw there was a cup of hot coffee on his desk. He took his coat off and put his briefcase down beside his desk when there was a knock at the door, it was Sharpe.

'Good morning Conor. I hope you don't mind me making you a coffee and using your computer. I wanted to get a head start'.
'No problem Calum. Still not got an office then?' said Marks as he thought to himself Sharpe really does live up to his name. Every day he turns up for work, he's the first man in, he's the smartest dressed man in the building, he works hard and he's always smiling. Police Scotland couldn't pick a better poster boy.
'Well I'm apparently getting the office next to the Super's (DS Black) but there finishing painting it today so I should be in it tomorrow.'

'That's good. How did you get in here?'

'Ann let me in. I asked her.'

'No problem as long as you were in when she cleaned, it's not that I think she'd do anything untoward but there is a lot of confidential information in here' said Marks before he took a mouthful of his coffee' .

'We were the same in Glasgow, cleaners only got in when senior staff were in. I made sure I was here the whole time she was in. Any word on Beaumont?'

Marks was still drinking his coffee, 'mmm. That coffee's great have you put extra sugar in?'

'I put a bit of caramel flavouring in.'

'Caramel. That's the best coffee I've had. To answer your question, we're no further forward re Beaumont's whereabouts. But I'm going to contact the intelligent unit to see where we are regarding Beaumont's mobile phone. Hopefully, it will have pinged (been located) nearby and contact his bank to see if there has been any activity on the account' said Marks.

'Well here's hoping.'

'I take it there was nothing major overnight?'

'No just run of the mill stuff.'

'Ok. Keep me updated about DC's Sharma and Munro's enquiries.'

'No problem. What office are they working from today?' asked Sharpe.

'I'll need to check with licensing, I think they're in today so they might need to work from the Fraud office, on the fourth floor. It's only Anne Chisholm that works there now and I believe she's on holiday for two weeks, but I'll let you know.'

'Great thanks' said Sharpe before he headed off to the CID office to give the teams their briefing for the day.

'Good morning' said a softly spoken woman. No mention of what office you'd reached. But Marks knew he'd reached the right office.'

'Good morning. It's DCI Conor Marks here. Has there been any progress regarding the Beaumont mobile phone enquiry?'

'Yes sir, it came through about five minutes ago.'

'Unfortunately, the last time it was used as far as we can tell was on Thursday morning in Aberdeen when he paid for a room at the Hilton Hotel for two nights totalling £178.'

'Two nights, are you sure? His wife thought he'd be away for three nights.'

'Definitely two nights sir.'

'And there's been nothing else?'

'Not a thing.'

'Can you let me know if there's any other activity on the card?'

'Will do.'

'That'll be great but hopefully we won't need it. Thanks for that.'

Sharpe had gone into a meeting, but he had asked Sharma and Munro to check in with Marks before they settled into a desk and started working for today.

Marks was in the process of checking the duty sheets to ensure the Fraud office would be free when Sharma and Munro knocked on the door.

'Come in' said Marks.

Sharma and Munro entered and stood waiting on Marks finishing his phone call.

Marks was on the phone. 'That's great thanks.'

'Good Morning Angela, Mike. Good news, I've got you guys your own office for two weeks and I've also managed to obtain the use of a car for the coming week too.'

'Excellent, thanks sir' said Sharma.

'I've compiled a number of tasks to be done regarding the missing person report. However, it isn't on the system because if I had put it on the system some people would get access to it, and I don't want anyone that's not necessary to the investigation getting access. That's even if I classed it as confidential. So update the reports on the computer then save it on the S drive and send it to me once you've finished for the day. In the meantime if you could keep me and DCI Sharpe up-to-date with how you're getting on that'd be great.'

'Ok sir' replied Munro before he and Sharma left.

Marks was worried. Beaumont had only paid for two nights stay in Aberdeen and yet, assuming Louise hadn't made a mistake, he was away three nights. So where was he planning on spending the third night? Had he got himself into trouble? Was he supposed to stay at another hotel in another town or city? Has he got himself a girlfriend or a boyfriend? Was he lying injured somewhere? Was he in hospital? Only Beaumont would know but with his phone appearing to be off, the battery disconnected and no further transactions on his bank card they were running out of ways to locate Beaumont. Marks always worked with the idea that you hope for the best but prepare for the worst.

Marks checked in with Sharma and Munro to see where they were in their list of enquiries. He was impressed with the number of tasks they'd got through. But it seemed they too were having no luck.

Marks had finished speaking to Sharma and Munro and had returned to the CID office when Sharpe came into the office and commanded everyone's attention. There had been a murder. Not much was known about the circumstances as details were still coming in but as is standard practice when a murder is discovered everything else gets dropped, at least for most. Sharma and Munro were still tasked with locating Beaumont.

Details were filtering through about the murder. There had been a call made to police by the downstairs neighbour of a man well known to police, Alan Stark. The neighbour contacted police because he believed blood was coming through his hallway ceiling from the flat above. Uniformed officers attended and went to see this neighbour.

The first officers called to the address weren't overly concerned because they believed it would be spilt paint or a leaky pipe that had discoloured water coming from it. However, when they checked the man's ceiling, they found that it was blood. Both the officers looked at each other. They knew this meant two things. One there was a dead body in the flat above and two, for the blood to have seeped into the downstairs flat meant the body had been there for at least for four or five days.

They made their way to the upstairs flat. With every stair they climbed their mood deepened. When they got to the front door, they lifted the letterbox to knock at the door. That's when they got a whiff of the stench of the body. That easily identifiable smell of death. They knocked on the door, out of habit. There was no reply. There was no need to knock again. The smell of death is one police officer get used to very quickly, and unfortunately is not one you forget. Any police officer will tell you that there have been times when they've been able to smell death even when they're not around a dead body. One of the officers tried the door handle. The door was unlocked. The opened it slowly identifying themselves as police officers as they were overcome with the smell of death. They were confronted by a scene that wouldn't have looked out of place in a Quentin Tarantino film.

The officer that had opened the door stood for what seemed like an eternity but, was no more than a few seconds looking at the scene, whilst his brain took a few seconds to process what he was seeing. His partner couldn't stomach what she had seen and ran to the downstairs landing where she threw up. He saw the body of a male he recognised as the occupier Alan Stark. He was lying on his back in a pool of blood. His face and body were covered in blood. The officer never entered the flat. There was no need to. The man was dead and quite clearly had been for several days. He opted to stay at the edge of the door. But he could see Stark had no top on, no socks or shoes on. The hall had blood on the walls and on the ceiling.

All the local officers knew Alan Stark. He was in his early 30's, muscular, was a known drug dealer, was very aggressive towards police and was known to fight police officers. He was also known to have weapons stashed around the flat so that he could protect himself anywhere in the house.

As a result of this police officers were warned prior to attending at his flat not to attend on their own but in at least a pairing. It was normal for two officers to attend a call at his flat whilst others stood by outside the flat just in case he kicked off.

The senior of the two uniformed police officers stood guard at the flat until a senior officer attended. The first officer there was DCI Sharpe. He had attended with DS Bailey. He was experienced in leading murder investigations and knew that the preservation of evidence was critical. He opened the front door and saw the bloodied corpse. He saw no benefit to entering any further and compromising potential evidence. He returned to his car whilst awaiting SOCO (Scenes of Crime Officers) because he didn't have a protective suit to put on.

Whilst he waited patiently, he asked that a control room operator carry out police checks on Alan Stark to ascertain if he had any known viruses such as HIV or Hepatitis. After all, he was aware that there was a lot of blood in the flat and he didn't want to expose any officer to these risks. If it transpired that Stark had HIV or Hepatitis, then police would have to attend at the flat below and inform the gentleman who called police that he may need part of the ceiling renewed.

Sharpe was informed Stark was thought to have had Hepatitis C, but they would need to have this confirmed through deceased's medical records.

Dr Dempster, the force pathologist attended.

Sharpe introduced himself 'Good morning, I'm DCI Calum Sharpe. Dr Dempster isn't it?'
 'Yes that's correct Chief Inspector, call me Lynne' as she shook Sharpe's hand and smiled.
 'The deceased is lying in the hall on his back covered in blood. We haven't been in the flat, so we don't know any more now apart from we believe deceased had Hepatitis C. We're waiting on SOCO to arrive because we don't have paper suits in the car.'
 'Ok. I'll wait in the car' said the doctor.

Minutes later SOCO arrived and Dr Dempster, Sharpe, Bailey and the two SOCO's put on their protective paper suits. DC Mason started filming the front of the close, through the close, up the stairs where they found blood on one of the stair handrails. They carefully covered this so that no-one tampered with it until they were ready to take a sample of this blood. They also found three faint partial footprints on the landing outside of Starks flat leading to the stairwell and on the stairs.

Sharpe and Bailey saw that there were no marks on the outside of Starks door.
 'It doesn't look like entry was forced sir' said Bailey.

'No it doesn't. He must have either let them in, they had a key or maybe he doesn't lock his door?' said Sharpe.

'Make a point of emailing all officers who have attended here asking them if they know if deceased locked his door or not.'

'Ok sir.'

They opened the door. Sharpe looked at where the blood on the carpet was before placing metal foot plates on the carpet for them to walk in the hall without trampling on the evidence.

Once this was done Dr Dempster assessed the body to try and give some indication as to how and when the victim was murdered. But the body was so badly beaten, slashed and stabbed that she couldn't give an initial cause of death. She determined that the cause of death was through blunt force trauma but said she couldn't give the exact cause of death until she had carried out a post-mortem.

Sharpe, Bailey and the SOCO's then got on with the task of collecting evidence.

The hall was long, narrow and had several doors leading into other rooms in the flat.

Now that they had filmed deceased's body in situ, they began systematically searching the flat for forensic evidence. Martin continued filming whilst DCI Sharpe narrated what they were seeing.

The first door on the left was a small bedroom. It was decorated with white wallpaper and painted over with beige pain. The room was clean, neat and tidy. Nothing appeared to be touched here.

The next door they reached was on the right side of the hall. It was the kitchen. There appeared nothing of note in the kitchen, at least to Bailey. She saw that like the small bedroom, the kitchen was clean, neat and tidy. Everything seemed to have its place. However, Sharpe pointed out to anyone watching the filming of the scene that there was a block of kitchen knives on the worktop with one knife missing. SOCO's dusted for prints. They uplifted some fingerprints from the knife block, the kitchen worktop and from the light switch. Could this be the murder weapon? If it was, has the murderer picked up the knife with the intention of murdering Stark or did Stark have the knife with him in the living room for some reason? Was he expecting trouble? All questions Sharpe and his team would endeavour to find out.

Sharpe's phone rang, it was DC Davie, he told Sharpe that he had been asked by DCI Marks to look at the latest intelligence the police had on Stark to see if this could shed any light on who killed Stark.

Davie told Sharpe that there were numerous intelligence entries which indicated Stark was involved in dealing drugs for Sean Murray. That he was frequently in possession of knives when out and about. There was also intelligence to suggest Stark had a safe in his bedroom where he would keep his money and drugs.

Sharpe and Bailey were surprised they hadn't found any drugs or drugs paraphernalia in the house, but this could be because the drugs, money and drugs paraphernalia were in the safe. They went looking for the safe in the bottom of a wardrobe. Sure enough under a mountain of clothes they found as the intelligence indicated, the safe. Neither Sharpe nor Bailey knew anything about safes but this safe had a digital keypad and was locked. This meant they would need a code to open it. They didn't have this; in fact, they didn't know if it was a 4 or 6 number pin code. Fortunately, it wasn't fixed to the wall or wardrobe. So they could take the safe with them to Headquarters. Where they would require the help of an expert on safes because they had no way of knowing the code.

Bearing in mind the intelligence they had on deceased, it was fair to assume that it was either money, drugs, or both in the safe. This would explain why they never found any drugs in the flat. They hadn't found any scales or a tick list either. Sharpe thought that this was strange because Stark was heavily involved in the drugs scene and that he may have been killed for what was in the safe. They, however, would not know this until they opened the safe.

Sharpe knew that there was recent intelligence suggesting that a drugs war was looming in Dundee between rival factions led by local hardman

George Douglas, and Sean Murray. Not only that but there was a gang thought to be from Liverpool who were trying to establish themselves in the area.

The fact that it was common knowledge Alan Stark dealt drugs for Sean Murray and he was now dead only added further credibility to the thought that a drugs war may have started or was about to start.

Unfortunately for Sharpe and his team this meant Stark may have had several enemies willing to kill him.
Once they finished at the scene Sharpe and Bailey returned to Headquarters but not before Sharpe walked around the area of the entrance to the close looking for drains where the knife may have been discarded. He knew he wouldn't be able to see the knife in the drains, if it was in one of the drains, but there may be blood on the drain and this would give an indication that the knife may be in that drain. He also wanted to see if there was any cctv near the area that may have caught the culprit coming or going from the scene.

Sharpe updated Marks whilst Bailey went to the incident room to write on the whiteboard deceased's details, when and where he was last seen and who he was with. Possible suspects and possible motives would also be written on a whiteboard; however this may be a long list.

Sharpe updated Marks regarding what he had found at locus. He was very confident that they would get a positive result from the scenes of crime evidence due to the volume of fingerprints lifted and from where they were lifted.

The SOCO's lifted numerous fingerprints from deceased's flat, and from numerous locations. They also lifted some partial shoe prints, blood from the handrails of the stairs, lots of blood from inside the flat, some hairs and fibres from deceased's tracksuit bottoms. As deceased had a criminal record his fingerprints would be on record so they would easily be able to confirm if any of the fingerprints found belonged to him. Hopefully, the person or persons responsible would also be known to police on the DNA database.

They were positive that with the number of items they had extracted from the crime scene that they would have the killer's DNA. The only disappointing aspect of the day was that they hadn't recovered the murder weapon.

Robbie arrived at Sean's home address. He was one of only a few people who knew where he stayed. Sean did all his drug dealing from a flat he rented out because he didn't want anyone connecting his own flat to his drug dealing. He told everyone he was a professional punter, and he owned a taxi firm. A business he used as a front to launder the cash he earned through his drug dealing. He was aware he was making too much money from his drug dealing to this attribute it all to his taxi's, after all he only had three which is why he came up with the idea of being a professional gambler.

This however meant he had to spend most of his week in the bookies in order to launder most of his money earned through selling drugs. Sean knew that the Proceeds of Crime Act 2002 allowed police to confiscate monies they believed had been earned through criminal activities, but that it had to be at least £1,000 that a person had to have in their possession. This is why Sean never had more than nine hundred pounds on him at any one time. He had his gambling down to a fine art. It was a complex system he had but one that he had worked on for some time and one where he couldn't lose. However this meant several journeys a day to different bookies because all the transactions in a bookie is electronically tagged and Sean knew this. Even the betting terminals where you can play any number of games, including roulette, are monitored electronically. The bookies can tell how much money you've put into the machines, what you've bet on and how much you've won. This was too detailed for Sean because the if the police investigated his finances, they would see exactly how much he's spending, and he would have to say where he'd got the money from. However, if he went into different premises, he could say he went into one bookmaker and placed whichever bet won. Unless they had him under surveillance, he wouldn't get caught.

He also had measures in place with regards to the flat where he dealt drugs that would make it very difficult for police to catch him in the act. For one, he seldom touched the drugs. He paid people to do his dirty work for him and he paid them well because he didn't want people talking to the police.

He'd been involved in the drugs scene for some time and was very clued up on who's dealing for who and what drugs they deal in. He was aware that whilst he controlled the East of the city, the West of the city was controlled by George Douglas.

Sean's close was secured by secure entry. However his name wasn't on the list of flats. Instead Sean's buzzer had a paw print on it. That way, only people who knew Sean would know what button to press to ask to be let in the close and he made sure not to give his address to anyone.

Robbie knocked on the door. Sean let him in. Robbie could tell straight away something was wrong. 'Have you heard about Starky?' said Sean as the two of them walked into the living room.
  'No, what's up? Did he get raided?' said Robbie as he took a seat on one of the armchairs.
  'No. He's been killed.'
  'What, when, what happened?'
  'Don't know much at the minute. All I know is he was stabbed in his flat. They've cordoned off the flat.'
  'Stabbed. Who the fuck is daft enough to go to Starky's and stab him? It must have been somebody out his face coz Starky's a hard bastard.'
  'No idea. Somebody's gonna pay for this. I've already put the word out a grand to the first person that tells me who dunnit.'
  'Fuck. Starky was a good guy. A fucking nutter but he was a good guy. Do you think somebody tried to rip him off?'
  'It's possible. But as you said who's daft enough to do that?'
  'The only person who's got the contacts to do that is Douglas, but I thought everyone was happy with the deal we made.'
  'So did I if he's trying to take over our turf then there'll be trouble. I've built up a good thing in the West side of Dundee.'
Well, let's wait a minute. We need to think this through. Why would anyone want to start a war with us and why would they start with Starky, I

mean there's easier targets. Starky would be the last one of our dealers I'd go for if it were me.'

'Yeah I agree.'

'Do you think it's possible it could be another squad trying to move in on our turf?' said Robbie.

'S'pose it could be. I mean didn't Sampson, you know that guy from Perth we met on Saturday night, say at the weekend that a few guys from Liverpool were asking him questions about where to get gear and that?'

'Now that you mention it, I remember him saying something about Liverpudlians. Hopefully, they're not trying to get into Dundee because they're seriously well organised.'

'I know. Let's find out what we can about Starky's murder before we do anything.'

'Ok. The weekend was mental. I've never drunk that much in my life.'

'Me neither, nor that stuff we took was unbelievable.'

Robbie smiled and nodded his head 'Aw man. I've never felt like that before. Not sure I'll do it again though. I mean as good as it was it's taken me days to fe#el back to normal.'

Sean laughed 'Yeah, it was pretty strong.'

Chapter 5

WEDNESDAY

The post-mortem was attended by Detective Chief Inspector Calum Sharpe, Detective Sergeant Bailey, the Procurator Fiscal and of course Dr Dempster, who would be performing the post-mortem, and her faithful assistant Tommy Turner, who would be videoing the procedure, now that he had prepared the tools for Dr Dempster to use.

Tommy was considered a strange guy by most people. But Sharpe found Tommy very polite and pleasant. Sharpe wondered if it was the fact that Tommy was a hard worker who wasn't one for small talk.

What people didn't know about Tommy was that he was in two bands, one as the drummer and the other as the lead guitarist, and he was quite the showman. To the few people who knew him he was Clark Kent by day and Superman by night. At work Tommy was quiet, hard-working and came across as being a bit creepy, probably more to do with the job than anything else. But away from it, he was considered by his friends as being a guitar legend, who had quite a following on the local band circuit. From the few that really knew him he was thought to be a very thoughtful and considerate guy who in his spare time helped raise money for charity.

This was a side of him that very few police officers had seen. Dr Dempster knew him better than anyone else in the police and she was fiercely loyal to Tommy. A trait she showed one day when a constable thought it was okay to bad mouth him in her presence. She left him, and everyone else speechless when she erupted in a foul-mouthed tirade at the young cop.

Dr Dempster began the post-mortem. She talked about what she was doing and seeing as she was conducting the post-mortem whilst her assistant Tommy filmed the process.

She began by taking scrapings from underneath deceased's nails. As is common practice when stabbings are thought to be the cause of death, Dr

Dempster started where she thought the deepest cut was, measuring the length and depth of the cut. She noted that some of the stab wounds were antemortem, some were perimortem and others post-mortem. Dr Dempster was always fully aware of the need to explain in layman's terms what the medical terminology was. Antemortem is, as expected wounds inflicted before death. Perimortem is wounds inflicted just before death and post-mortem is obviously wounds inflicted after death. There was no doubt in her mind that this was overkill, and the fifteen stab wounds after death proved that. Dr Dempster noted that there were twenty-one stab wounds on deceased's body in total and that he had been stabbed at least once in the heart and had been slashed four times across the face. One of these slashes had slit his eyeball. She concluded from the shape of stab wounds that the murder weapon was a large knife, at least 20 cm in length and one that had one straight edge and one smooth curved edge. She stated that the murder weapon was probably a kitchen knife.

Dr Dempster concluded that Stark had sustained defence wounds on his arms and fingers. She found that the stab wound through the heart was what had killed him. He died instantly from this wound.

She found that Stark had injuries to his knuckles and that may have been due to him possibly trying to fight off the killer or killers before being overcome by his injuries. She told Sharpe that due to Stark having sustained defence cuts on his hands and arms, there is a very strong possibility that the killer would also have sustained cuts to his hands, when Stark had tried grabbing the knife.

This could be very significant thought Sharpe because it means that some of the blood samples that the scenes of crime officers obtained from the flat could belong to the killers.

Sharpe knew this gave them another line of enquiry. He took note that he would have to task an officer to make enquiries at the local hospitals to check if anyone had visited Accident and Emergency with cuts to their hands. Under the circumstances it was highly likely that the killer would have had to seek medical attention.

Dr Dempster couldn't narrow down the time of death because of the circumstances in which it was found.

Sharpe knew through experience that the time of death in this case is something that will have to be narrowed down through good old-fashioned door to door enquiries and cctv footage, (If they had any).

Sharpe returned to his office after stopping of at Marks' office and updating him regarding the post-mortem. He tried to work how it may have played out in his mind. Stark answers the door. He either lets the people in, which would indicate he knows them, or they barge their way in. Being that he was killed in the hall, it's fair to say he probably didn't know his killers.

According to local police officers, Stark was known to fight with officers and could be quite a handful. He's young, tall and muscular and so it is also fair to assume that there were at least two killers. Who killed him could be one of the hardest questions to solve because he was a drug dealer who was known to be violent towards anyone who irked him? They had learned through replies to a city-wide email sent to local officers that Stark was known to be very security conscious. He made sure that his door was always locked, even during the day when he was in, in order to ensure he wasn't the victim of a sneak in theft, a police raid or being raided by another dealer. This told Sharpe that he must have answered the door to his killers.

Sharpe was also aware that there was intelligence to suggest there may be a drugs war between local drugs gangs and gangs looking to get themselves a foothold in the local drugs scene. He was hoping this wasn't the start of a drugs war because if it is, then they can expect more violence on the street.

Chapter 6

When Sharpe left Marks sat with his head in his hands at his desk with nothing but the ticking of his clock for company. He was exhausted. He took one of his tablets to give him an energy boost. He had numerous thoughts going through his mind, but they were all in relation to the missing Barry Beaumont. He sat motionless for about ten minutes before the tablet took effect and he gathered his composure.

Sharma, with help from DC Munro, had exhausted all lines of enquiry in their efforts to trace Barry Beaumont safe and well. Marks understood a missing person enquiry is fast moving, things are always changing, but he had hoped they would've at least contacted Beaumont to confirm if he was okay.

Disturbing news was coming in that a male had been found badly beaten in a wooded area of Drumgeith Park. DS Bailey knocked at Marks' door.
'Come in.'
'Sir reports are coming in that a male has been discovered in the wooded area of Drumgeith Park very badly beaten. There's no news of who he is, what happened, why he's there and how he got there?'
'Ok. Thanks Lisa, I'll send DC Sharma because she's got a job to do for me anyway.'
'Ok sir' said Bailey.

Marks contacted Sharma and told her he would print off a photo of Beaumont which was for her eyes only. She was to nip into his office and pick up this photo before making her way to Drumgeith Park. When she came into his office, Marks said if she identified the male as being Barry Beaumont, she had to let him know as soon as possible.'

DC Sharma drove up to Drumgeith Park as quickly as she could, bearing in mind she was in an unmarked car. If this is Beaumont, then it means at least he's safe now. It will also mean she can now join the rest of her team in the murder investigation. Sharma was a keen officer and gave one hundred percent effort and focus in everything she did.

Sharma soon realised that she had been given the keys to the oldest, most run-down unmarked police car the police had. Not only that but it was lunch time and all the schools were getting out which meant the quickest routes were now as slow as the other routes.

She arrived in the nick of time. The paramedics were about to take the male to hospital. Unfortunately, the male didn't have any identification on him, and he was unconscious. She couldn't get a good look at his face because the male had an oxygen mask on, but she was confident it wasn't Beaumont.

She checked the report to see if Barry Beaumont was wearing the same clothes as the male who had apparently been assaulted. No, he hadn't. She was aware however, that he hadn't been home for several days and may have had clothes like that in his suitcase.

She spoke to the uniformed police officers that had traced the male. But they had no idea how long he'd been there. She asked the officers if they had confirmed the identity of the male, but they hadn't managed this either because the male had no identification, no wallet, nothing.

Sharma updated Marks, who asked her to attend at the hospital and have it confirmed either way. Sharma attended at hospital and was informed by the doctors that the male, yet unknown, had to undergo surgery for a bleed on the brain. Sharma updated Marks again and was asked to return to

headquarters. A uniformed officer would attend when hospital staff informed them that he was out of surgery and able to talk.
Meanwhile back at headquarters detectives had left the office in their droves to carry our door to door enquiries in the block Stark was killed and any other flat or house that could see the entrance/exit to deceased's building or even into the flat.

They were checking to see if anyone in the vicinity had seen or heard any disturbance over the last week. They would also check for any private cctv in the area that may have caught the killer coming or going to the flat.

Sharpe envisaged a problem. How would they review the cctv footage? The cctv suite has been taken over by detectives trying to trace Barry Beaumont, but they had a brutal murder on their hands and whilst priority is always given to a murder investigation, the missing person on this occasion was one of their own.

Sharpe asked around to see if anyone were aware of any other cctv facilities that they could use to carry out their reviews. Fortunately, he was informed that there was a cctv suite in Forfar and although this would only allow one person to review one dvd at a time, there didn't appear to be any another alternative.

Sharpe was aware that DC's Sharma and Munro were still working on the Beaumont enquiry, but knew they generally finished at around 5pm. He decided that he would assign detectives to trawl through the piles of cctv footage they had in relation to the murder, and that they could use the cctv suite in Dundee to do that. If, the time came whereby Sharma, Munro or anyone else working on the missing person enquiry required the cctv suite for an urgent review, then he would allow them to use it.

So far Sharpe and his team knew that the last sighting they had of Alan Stark was 6 days before he was discovered, at around 8pm when he was seen by a neighbour walking into the close as they were coming out. This would have been Tuesday 14th August. The neighbour downstairs last heard something or someone in the flat last Wednesday 15th August, but he couldn't be sure of the time although it was in the early hours of the morning when he believes he heard someone walking about.

Sharpe chose to go with the sighting of Stark as the last time they knew he was alive because there is no way of knowing if the noise the neighbour heard was Stark. But he knew the absence of someone like Stark in the neighbourhood would not go unnoticed for too long. If he were a betting man, he would put his money on that they would be able to narrow down his time of death quite significantly through the cctv footage they had. Unfortunately, it was one of those jobs that can take some time.

Stark unfortunately wasn't close to any of his family that lived in Dundee. He hadn't seen his father since he was a child, his mother was dead, he had no brother or sisters. He did have an uncle in Dundee, but he never saw him. They didn't know if he had any other family members at this stage. It was beginning to look like they would need a friend of his to identify the body.

Sharma contacted Accident and Emergency before she finished to ask about the male that had been assaulted in Drumgeith park. She was informed that this male was a local man called Simon Taylor who they had recognised as being a drunk who had been conveyed up to Ninewells hospital on several occasions after falling over or fighting. He had a bleed on the brain, but they believed this was not caused by an assault.

Chapter 7

THURSDAY

Sharpe had finished the briefing, and everyone had their jobs for the day. Sharpe would continue to oversee everything from the incident room.

DC's Crichton and Milne had been tasked with tracking down available cctv footage before it gets wiped for good. Sharpe knew that most businesses that have cctv only retain the footage for 14 days, however due to amount of cctv footage around today, and the lack of review officers it would take more than 14 days to review all of it.

They started with the nearest businesses to the murder and worked outwards. Unfortunately, Starks' close did not have cctv. They spent the whole morning obtaining cctv from various premises but needed to narrow down the time Stark was last seen alive to the time he was discovered.

Uniform officers had been offered overtime, (a rare thing in the police these days) to entice them to assist CID with house to house enquiries. These efforts were being overseen by CID officers.

Whilst experienced detectives were tasked with speaking to family and friends, DS Budd was instructed to chase up the results of the Scenes of Crime analysis of the murder scene. The Scenes of Crime Officers took video footage of the scene, hundreds of pictures, dozens of samples of blood, footwear imprints, fingerprints, fibres, DNA, practically anything that had the slightest chance of providing them with evidence.

An expert safe cracker was due to attend headquarters too, in order to ascertain what was in the safe that belonged to Alan Stark. Sharpe wanted to oversee this.

The CID offices were almost empty such was the scale of the enquiry. DC Sharma remained due to her being assigned to the case of missing policeman Barry Beaumont.

House to house wasn't going particularly well. Sharpe suspected this was largely due to deceased's involvement in the drug scene. People knew if they said anything to police then that may have repercussions for them and possibly friends or family. Although the police weren't getting anyone to say in their official statements who was involved, they were telling officers that this was the start of a drugs war between three or four rival gangs for control of Dundee and its connecting towns.

Officers were receiving intelligence that George Douglas's gang and Sean Murrays' gangs had joined together in order to repel the Liverpudlian gang that were trying to muscle into the area. Murray and Douglas had decided to keep to their original plan, set months ago after long talks between the two gang leaders that Murray would be the main dealer for everything to the east of city whilst Douglas would control the west. They would share the city centre of Dundee. The intelligence was from three different sources so there was every likelihood that it was genuine.

However, it appeared that Alan Stark, who was dealing drugs on behalf of Sean Murray decided to rob the occupants of a nearby flat who he believed were stealing his trade. Not content with stealing their cash and drugs, they felt the need to hospitalise the two occupants, one of which is the cousin of Paul MacDonald, the notorious Liverpudlian drugs kingpin. Unfortunately, the drugs and money in this flat also belonged to MacDonald. The Liverpudlians were notorious for their level of violence towards anyone they thought had wronged them. Alan Stark found this out to his cost.

Although no-one knew the names of the people involved in the murder of Alan Stark, it was common knowledge this was the Liverpudlians laying down a marker to anyone thinking of taking them on. It was also a statement that they can get to anyone anywhere by murdering him in his flat.

The problem for Sharpe and his team of detectives was that they didn't know any names of the people involved. At least that was until DCI Marks received a brief, unexpected but welcome phone call from Garry Flynn, aka, Barry Beaumont.

Beaumont gave the safe word to Marks. Fortunately Black had told Marks what the safe word was.

Beaumont spoke quickly and quietly. He didn't say where he was, but he told Marks he believed his identity had been compromised. He didn't say how he thought this but did say there were only a handful of people knew his real identity and that it must have been someone with authority in the police. As a result of this, he was keeping a very low profile. He hadn't even contacted his wife but asked that Marks let her know he was okay before he hung up. The phone call lasted for less than twenty seconds.

Marks called Sharpe and they went together to see Black. Marks told them what Beaumont had said on the phone. Nobody had any idea who the leak was, then again, it could be someone within the Scottish Crime and Drug Enforcement Agency.

They discussed the best way forward and kept the details of their meeting strictly between them. They agreed not to let anyone know that Beaumont was alive, except for DC's Sharma and Munro. They were being tasked with joining up with the teams working on the murder enquiry, but they were informed that should the situation with Beaumont change, then they would be back on that enquiry in an instant.

Marks and Sharpe were returning to the CID office when Sharpe was contacted by a member of the public enquiry office. There was a Michael Watson, safe cracker at the front desk. Sharpe made his way down to the public enquiry office. The number of times he walked up and down those stairs in a day meant there was no need for him to join a gym. He'd recently added a fitness app to his phone which counted the number of steps he walked in a day. It was only dinnertime and he'd walked over three thousand steps.

Sally, a member of the public enquiry office told Sharpe, that Watson was the male standing with a large bag.

 'Good afternoon, I'm Detective Chief Inspector Calum Sharpe' as he stretched out to shake Watson's hand.
Watson shook his hand 'Michael Watson.'

'Follow me please. Do you think it'll take you a bit of time to get into it?'

'Not if they've given me the correct information over the phone.'

'Great. Through here' said Sharpe as he walked through the double swing doors and yet again, started to climb the stairs.

'I hope you don't mind but we'll need a statement from you when you've opened the safe whether there's something in it or not.'

'Yeah, I the person on the phone said that. That's ok.'

Sharpe noticed Watson wasn't very tall, he was stocky if not a bit overweight and was started to breathe heavily as they began to walk up the fourth set of stairs. He let out a deep breath.

'Tell you what, bugger walking up these stairs every day' said a red-faced Watson.

'It certainly keeps you fit' said Sharpe whilst he was hoping Mr Watson would make it to the room where the safe was because he didn't fancy giving this guy the kiss of life.

Watson said nothing but Sharpe thought this was because he couldn't catch his breathe. To make matters worse as he reached the top of the fourth set of stairs, the lift opened and out walked three women carrying their lunch. This drew a rather dirty look from Watson to Sharpe. Sharpe knew he was thinking why the hell did you take the stairs when there's a perfectly good lift?

Sharpe said 'through here' as he held the doors open for Watson. 'It's just around here.'

'Okay.'

Sharpe opened the door. There was nothing in this room but for the safe sitting on a table.

'Do you want a tea or coffee?' asked Sharpe.

'I'll have a white coffee, three sugars, ta.'

Sharpe left the room momentarily before returning. 'One of my detectives will bring your coffee through in a minute.'

'Great' said Watson as he began digging into his bag, pulling out various tools.

Sharpe waited until the young detective brought a coffee for each of them. Sharpe was keen to have the safe opened, but he didn't want to deprive Mr Watson of his reward for climbing the stairs.

He needn't have worried. Watson downed the coffee in a matter of seconds.
 'Aaaahhh. I needed that' said a relieved Watson.

Sharpe contacted SOCO to let them know the safe would be opened soon. Sharpe asked DC Davie to stay whilst the safe was opened to corroborate what was in the safe. He took this opportunity to remind Watson that he was needed to unlock the safe only. Under no circumstances, was he to touch anything? Watson had the safe unlocked within a matter of minutes. Sharpe, although he had no knowledge of the workings of a safe, was impressed.

Sharpe and the Davie put on gloves.

 'That's fine Mr Watson, thank you' said Sharpe as he opened the safe. 'Brilliant' said Sharpe his eyes focused on the pile of cash and bags of drugs in the safe. But that wasn't why Sharpe said brilliant. It was because he spotted what appeared to be a ledger. This he suspected would contain information about Stark's drug dealing, which may in itself provide police with people who had a motive to kill Stark.

DC Davie began taking a statement from Watson as they waited for SOCO. Once they arrived, they took the necessary photos. Watson was thanked for his time and then escorted from the building by Davie, who returned to the room, as instructed by Sharpe. Sharpe had waited for Davie to return before removing anything from the safe. Regardless of rank, the one thing no officer took any chances around was money. You couldn't leave your lunch lying around for too long or a tin of sweets because they'd be eaten by the time the next shift comes on duty. But money was a different story. You could leave a pound coin sitting on a desk and go back for it a week later and it won't have moved from its original spot. Any inference that money had gone missing would cause officers to be investigated. No one wanted that because Professional Standards could find dirt on anyone. Which was ironic in most officers opinions because the cops that usually worked in Professional Standards were usually the shadiest of cops. The ones with the most skeletons in the closet.

Sharpe took out the items from the safe as SOCO and Davie looked on.

First thing he took out was the large bag of white powder.

'That's got to be about a kilo of Coke there. That's gotta be worth about £50,000' said DC Mason,
(SOCO).
'I'm wondering if that's the drugs and cash Stark stole from the Liverpudlians' said Sharpe.
'It could be' said Mason.
'John (Davie) can you lodge all these items as productions in the meantime. Put them as belonging to Alan Stark. We'll need to apply to the court to have the drugs and the money confiscated as per the Proceeds of Crime Act.'
'No problem sir.'
Sam Mason began dusting the bag of drugs for fingerprints. 'Might be in luck here sir. I've got one full fingerprint here and a couple of partial fingerprints.
'Great. It'll probably be Stark's, but you never know, we could get lucky.'
They then systematically took all the items out of the safe, one at a time.

1. Large bag of white powder (Cocaine)
2. Small bag of brown powder (Heroin)
3. Ledger
4. Pen
5. Calculator
6. Scales
7. Clear bags
8. Pile of Money

Each item photographed, labelled and placed in production bags except for the money. This had to be dusted for prints, counted, put in a clear bag and every serial number of every note shown so that there was no mistaken how much money there was.

Sharpe knew this task alone would take some time, so left once it had been counted, but not before he looked through the ledger. This was a great find. It detailed who was owe Stark money for drugs. It was dated too.

£12,240 in £50, £20 and £10 notes.

DC's Davie and Mason were there over two hours doing this task alone.

Chapter 8

Louise Beaumont graduated from university with a first-class honours' degree in law. She would later become one of the most sought-after criminal lawyers in the land. Her profile shot up overnight when she somehow successfully defended Kenny Travis on a murder charge that most people thought he was banged to rights for. Travis would later tell some of his closest friends he had been preparing himself for being jailed for at least 10 years for culpable homicide. But somehow the jury returned a verdict of not proven. The prosecution was in disbelief at the outcome as was Travis.

Culpable homicide is the Scottish equivalent of manslaughter and is where the accused meant to harm the victim but not kill them. Louise Beaumont had successfully argued that it was no more than a fight between two healthy males in which one male died after, she argued, he tripped over his own feet after being punched, which is what led to him banging his head against a wall as he fell. There was no cctv to back this up and she managed to put enough doubt in the mind of the jury that they returned a verdict of not proven.

Of course there were occasions where it caused friction in the Beaumont household. She would always argue however, that if the police had done their job correctly then her clients would be found guilty, such is the nature of Scots Law, and it's need for evidence to be corroborated.

After serving her time working for a major law firm, she decided to start her own company. She appeared to live a good life, although she worked an incredible number of hours especially in the early days of her business. No one could say that she didn't deserve what she had because she worked extremely hard to provide a good life for her and her husband. Not that he was work shy, they two were alike. He worked long hours in the police. Ironically, it was due to the number of hours she worked that her friends decided to set her up on a date with Barry. She hadn't had a date for months and her friends knew this. They thought if she could meet someone, she would focus on something else other than her work. She reluctantly agreed to the double date with her friend Rachel and her then boyfriend John.

Rachel's current boyfriend John was friends with Barry.

Louise and Barry's relationship took a little time to develop due to their work commitments but once they began spending more time with each other their relationship grew quickly. Within three years of starting their relationship, Louise and Barry were married. During the next few years they worked hard and saved hard. They hoped to buy the house of their dreams in which they could raise a family. There hard work was rewarded with a promotion for both Louise and Barry. Life was good. They holidayed abroad twice a year, drove nice cars and wore expensive clothes.

Louise and Barry never had children, but whether it was a decision not too or was because they couldn't no one knew, and they never discussed it.

Louise eventually opened her own law firm whilst Barry changed departments a few times, taking time to work in CID, the drugs branch and intelligence unit of the police.

Barry and Robbie had a good relationship until Robbie's gambling addiction took over. Barry had given Robbie money after he'd lost his entire month's wages in an afternoon at the bookies. However, it was the fact that Robbie did the same again the following month that irked Barry. When Barry said he wouldn't give him or lend him money because he feared he would do the same again, Robbie had no choice but to tell his then girlfriend Sarah what he'd done.

Unfortunately, she had experienced similar problems with her last boyfriend and couldn't cope with Robbie doing the same and she left him. Robbie was devastated and he blamed Barry for this.

Louise and Robbie had always got on well together and so the fractious relationship between Barry and Robbie saddened her. She had always found Robbie to be a good guy, who worked hard, albeit she believed he could have achieved a lot more in his life had he had Barry's work ethic. There was also a mutual attraction between them, which hadn't gone unnoticed by some of her friends. Barry however seemed oblivious to this.

They had never told Barry because they feared how it may affect their relationship's, but Robbie and Louise had spent one drunken weekend together prior to Louise and Barry getting together. Nothing came of it probably because they were both young. Robbie, who is 4 years younger than Barry and Louise, was only eighteen at the time. But Robbie, if he were being honest with himself, had on occasions, wondered what life would be like if he and Louise had got together.

He knew nothing could ever come of it, unless circumstances changed dramatically and Barry was out of the picture. But this didn't change how he felt. Sometimes he thought that it was just his luck that he met her at the wrong time.

He had on one occasion even thought of telling Louise about Barry's secret, but he felt he couldn't do that despite him having what he was wanting. They were brothers after all. Besides it's bound to come out sooner rather than later thought Robbie.

Chapter 9

George Douglas is the eldest of son of George Douglas Snr and Sharon Douglas. He has three brothers and two sisters. Although George Snr was a mechanic by day and a doorman at the local pub at the weekends there wasn't a lot of money in the household.

George Jnr considered himself the luckiest of the children because he was the oldest. This meant that he got new clothes when he needed them whereas his brother tended to get his old clothes. On occasions he got handed down clothes from his big cousin Frank, but due to George Jnr being taller and more muscular than Frank by the time he was 9 (Frank was 12) this didn't last long.

The Douglas' had a big family, George Snr had six children, his brothers Frank and John had four each, Frank had three boys, one girl and John had three girls and one boy. Of course this meant that although they didn't receive a great deal at Christmas, or on birthdays (having such a big family meant that it was someone's birthday every other week) but they were always happy family events. Christmas dinners were like military planned operations. Everyone had a job even the youngest of all the children Katy, she had to put Christmas crackers at all the plates. When George Jnr thought about how his mum and dad coped, he wondered how they never cracked under the pressure.

George Jnr believed that his parents' strict discipline and the regimented routines they had helped install the hard-working attitude they all had. Although he would be the first to admit that neither him nor his siblings were ever likely to become Brain Surgeons they could never be faulted for effort.

Fortunately because there was so many of the Douglas' they never got into much bother. George Jnr however was the exception. He was always in some sort of bother, usually fighting. He was naturally quite a big strong lad, like his dad and he had his dad's temper.

Well they say ginger haired folk are fiery and in George's case, they were right. By the time he was sixteen he had been involved in so many fights that he had gained a reputation as a hard man. This didn't sit well with some people including Barry Hamilton, who despite being twenty was one of the main men of the Hilltoon Huns, a local gang from the Hilltown area who frequently fought with people from Kirkton. (Where George originated from)

One day Hamilton saw George walking through the Hilltown on his own. During these days when gang culture was rife Hamilton saw this as an act of bravado from George, and one that his ego couldn't take. What would other gangs think if they knew a sixteen-year-old walked through the Hilltown without anyone doing anything. Hamilton, like George, was a big lad and feared no-one.
Hamilton shouted on George. George heard him but chose to ignore him. He knew what was about to happen. He wasn't scared, in fact he was more relaxed fighting than he was speaking in front of a crowd of people, but he was dressed in his best gear and was on his way to meet a girl for their first date. He kept on walking, at least until Hamilton realised, he was not getting a reaction and stupidly started making remarks about George's mum.

Unfortunately for him he got a reaction from George. But it certainly wasn't the one he was expecting. Yes, he'd heard George could fight but he knew he could fight too. However, he either underestimated George's fury over his comments or he overestimated his own fighting ability. He saw an enraged George turn to face him. By this time some of the local Hilltown lads had come into the street. Hamilton threw the first punch, catching George on jaw. He'd got him a cracker but was shocked when there was no reaction from George. George grabbed Hamilton by the jumper and headbutted him shattering his nose, then he punched Hamilton three times in the face. Hamilton fell to the ground. His face now covered in blood his cream jumper highlighting just how much blood was pouring out of his nose and mouth.

However, it was what happened next that resulted in George getting a fearsome reputation as someone is not argued with. Although fighting was common back then, it was uncommon for someone to continue to hit a person once they were on the ground, it was an unwritten rule you left them to nurse their injuries. George's rage knew no bounds however, he stamped on Hamilton's head a number of times until he was unconscious even then he only stopped because two old women screamed when they saw what was happening and this seemed to bring George out of the rage he was in. Despite there were about ten Hilltown lads in the street at the time, no-one was willing to step in and help Hamilton. Such was the fear of a similar reaction by George to them.

When George thinks back to this day, he's thankful two women screamed, otherwise he may have killed Hamilton and ruined both their lives.

When George Snr heard about what happened he had words with George Jnr. Whilst he appreciated that Hamilton should have expected a reaction from him, he thought he had went too far, as he pointed out to George Jnr, he could so easily have been facing a murder charge. The fact the police were never involved stunned even George Snr. Apparently, some of the boys that witnessed the fight, took Hamilton to one of their houses until he recovered so that his parents wouldn't see him in such aa state. The incident had a profound effect on Hamilton to the extent that he never made any complaint to police for fear of reprisals.

Although George Jnr wanted to make his dad proud, he couldn't help but get into trouble. It seemed to follow him. But if he was being honest with himself, he enjoyed the rush he got from fighting, drinking, taking drugs, and generally doing what he wanted. Unfortunately, because of the incident with Hamilton where he was too scared to go to the police, this just allowed him to think he could do whatever he wanted. Even his dad talking to him and sharing his brushes with the police, it never stopped George cascading down the slippery slope to crime.

George Snr was no angel by any means but even he knew George Jnr was on road to becoming a big time criminal. He had hoped George and his brothers would become professional sportsmen. George though didn't have the temperament to be a football player. On the very day two scouts had come to see him, he knocked out an opponent who he felt had deliberately fouled him. This naturally resulted in him getting sent off, receiving a ten-match ban and scouts everywhere being put off signing him. He never played again.

Two of his brothers played rugby for Scotland whist his youngest brother was a talented boxer but had gotten his girlfriend pregnant and decided to get a job to provide for his family. The day his brother told his parents his girlfriend was pregnant and that he was giving up his dream to provide for them was one of the saddest and proudest moments in his parents' lives. They were disappointed for Graham but proud of the choice he made.

George Jnr wasn't sure if his parents had ever been or would ever be proud of him. After all, they blamed him for the death of his oldest son and their eldest grandson David Douglas. Douglas however blamed Barry Beaumont because he was the officer in charge of the case that got David Douglas sent to prison. David had always had depression, even from a young age his mother and father always kept a close eye on how he was feeling. When he was 17, he tried to take an overdose. Fortunately for him a dog walker stumbled across him a short time after he had taken the overdose. They performed CPR and this along with the prompt response from the Paramedics saved his life.

However, six weeks into his five-year sentence for being caught in possession of over one hundred thousand pounds worth of Cocaine he hung himself in his cell.

Douglas was devastated. He vowed he would never forget what Beaumont had done and that he'd one day he'd have his revenge.

George Douglas' parents felt their sacrifices and efforts to raise their children to do the right thing had been wasted, at least on George, after he had turned to crime. He would always claim trouble followed him and so there was no escape from it, but the reality was he got a kick out of being able to do whatever he wanted whenever he wanted. He also found that when you're top of the tree, crime pays.

Although he had his fingers in a lot of pies and was known to be a career criminal, he'd never spent time in jail. He put this down to a combination of things. Luck. He was always nowhere to be seen when houses got raided, people got beat up or drug deals went down. He also had a very good lawyer. On the rare occasion he was linked to crimes that would ordinarily see people jailed, his lawyer somehow got him off. As a result, it caused some underworld figures to suspect Douglas had dirt on senior police officers and judges or was providing them with information about other crime lords. Not that anyone would confront him about this.

Chapter 10

WEDNESDAY

Sean phoned Robbie, 'you busy?'
 'Not really, what's up?'
 'George Douglas phoned me, wants to meet and I'm not meeting him alone, so I'm asking you Cammy and Cammy's pal Hunter to come along for back up.'
 'Why are you meeting up with him?'
 'I need to find out who murdered Starky. I know he won't admit it even if it was him but if I can look into his eyes I'll know if it was him.'
 'You need to be careful; Douglas will be a handful for anyone, even you. He's big, strong and he's very well connected. 'What you gonna do if he says it was him who ordered the hit on Starky?'
 'Haven't given it a thought coz there's no way he'd admit it, besides, I've asked around and no-one seems to know anything about it. I figured even if it were one of Douglas' gang, people would be talking, and I'd find out.'
 'That's true. But if it wasn't him then who else?'
 'I don't know but I was speaking to Conzo and he heard that Starky and a couple of his mates smashed their way into a guy called Tony's flat, who stays in Nelson Street, leathered the two guys that were in the flat and stole their stash and about ten grand in cash.'
 'How do they know that?'
 'Apparently one of the guys, who's always broke, (Goofy) has been seen in Dundee city centre flashing the cash. Not just that but after he'd had a

few to many pints he started bragging about how he and his mates did the neighbourhood a favour by robbing a drug dealer.'

'Really' said a stunned Sean. 'Never heard of a guy called Goofy, have you?'

'Yeah, I bumped into him once, he was scrounging in the High Street with Davie Day. I'd won a few hundred in the bookies so I gave Davie twenty quid. If I remember correctly, he was from the west coast, Kilmarnock or Ayr someplace like that.'

'Don't suppose you know where he stays now?'

'Nah. But I'll put the word out we're looking for him.'

'What the fuck was Starky thinking? He can't be short of cash. Do you know this Tony? Can't say I've heard of anyone that deals from Nelson Street called Tony.'

'You knew Starky as well as me, fuck knows what possessed him to do that. Then again, he always was a fucking nutter. Who knows, maybe the guy owed him money.'

'That's probably what got him killed.'

'It makes sense right enough, but if the guy was dealing, and Douglas didn't know about it, then that would mean he's tied in with another squad.'

'Could be the Liverpudlians?'

'Now that would make sense. He tans one of their dealers for ten large and a load of gear. They find out and kill him. Not only do they sort out the guy who ripped them off, but they send a message that if anybody fucks with them, they'll end up like Starky.'

'Yeah. I hope you're wrong. I don't fancy taking on the Liverpudlians.'

'Me neither. George Douglas and his crew would be tough enough to sort out, never mind the Scousers. Well are you able to come to this meet?'

'Of course. Where and when?'

'If you can pick me up outside the bookies, at about two o'clock then we'll pick up Cammy and his mate Hunter before we go to the meet. We've to be at the top of the Law hill for half two.'

'Strange place to meet.'

'Douglas says it's so we can see if anybody's watching.'

'Good idea actually.'

'Well I'll see ye at two.'

'Cool. See you then.'
'See ye mate.'

Two o'clock on the dot Robbie picked up Sean, who put a bag in the boot of the car before getting in. They discussed their options whilst they drove to Cammy's flat to pick up him and Hunter.
 'Arite mate' said Sean as he got in the car.
 'Good. You?'
 'Aye arite.'
 'Where we going?'
 'I said we'd pick up Cammy and Hunter up outside the shops on Douglas Road.'
 'Ok.'
 'Who's this Hunter?'
 'Cammy's pal. Cammy says he's sound and always up for a fight. That's good enough for me.'
 'Wonder what Douglas wants.'
 'We'll find out soon enough' said Sean.'
 'Maybe he wants to set the record straight about Starky.'
 'Maybe.'
 'What if he admits his squad killed him.'
 'We can second guess him all day, but we'll see soon enough.'
 'You don't seem too concerned either way.'
 'I'm not, coz we'll deal with whatever its is.'
 'Have you got something planned? Coz you seem too fucking calm mate.'

Sean looked at Robbie and smiled smugly, like he knew he was in control of the situation, and that whatever the situation is he's got it sorted.

Robbie pulled up outside the shops in Douglas Rd as Cammy and Hunter were coming out of the newsagents.

 'Arite guys' said Sean. Robbie thought Sean sounded quite quiet and calm which wasn't like him. Whatever Sean had planned, was making Robbie nervous. He'd known Sean for a long time and any time he thought there was the potential for violence, he was always the one laughing and joking like it didn't bother him one bit. It wasn't that Sean was trying to give the impression he wasn't scared when he was, he genuinely enjoyed a fight and had no fear of anything or anyone. When he got started, he was a fucking madman. He didn't seem to feel pain like other people.

Robbie recalled when him and Sean as well as about twenty others went out for a stag do. Naturally, they got extremely drunk. They ended up getting into a fight in a nightclub. The doormen split the fight up, but Sean didn't realise at first that it was the doormen who were breaking it up and he headbutted one of them. Of course this meant the rest of the doormen went to protect their own, as you do. Sean ended up fighting with five of them, and none of these guys were small. They were all big guys and Sean and a couple of the doormen ended up on the ground. The doormen who were on their feet started kicking Sean in the body and head. Sean was laughing, shouting 'C'mon, is that all you've got'. Even when they were carrying him out the club, he was trying to kick and punch them. He was enjoying it. That's when Robbie realised Sean really did have issues.

'Arite guys. This is Hunter' said Cammy.
'Pleased to meet ye Hunter' said Sean 'Thanks for coming along today. I've no idea what's gonna happen. Probably nothing. Then again it could end up being one big brawl'
'That's alright with me' said Hunter in this thick Highland accent.
'Cool' said a smiling Sean.
Robbie didn't say anything but kept on driving.

They were almost there. Robbie started driving up Hill Street when Sean told him to pull in before he turned into Law Crescent and up the Law Hill.

He pulled in and Sean didn't say anything but got out of the car and went to the boot. He took the bag out that he had placed in the boot when Robbie picked him up. He got back in the front seat and opened the bag.

'Right lads, take what you want just in case all hell breaks loose. At that, he took out two knuckledusters and put one in each of his side pockets before passing the bag back to Cammy and Hunter. Robbie didn't see what they took out of the bag. But he guessed it wasn't a sports drink.

Cammy handed the bag back to Sean.

'What do you want Robbie?'
'What have you got?'
'Knife, machete, knuckleduster, nunchuks, hammer, crowbar or baseball bat. What do you want?'
'I'll take the crowbar'
'Good choice' said an excited Sean.
'Stick that up yer sleeve, so they don't see it, and if it goes pear shaped then smash anyone who isn't in this car'
Robbie nodded. He never let on, but he was bricking it. (Shitting himself with fear) He'd been big fights before but not where everyone is tooled up.'

They drove up to the top of the Law Hill. Douglas was already there. He was sitting in a transit van with one guy sitting in the passenger seat. There was one other vehicle, another van. But there didn't appear to be anyone in it that they could see anyway.

'Keep yer eyes peeled guys. He's probably got three or four guys in the back of the transit' said Sean.   'Robbie leave the keys in the ignition and get out with me.'
'Ok' said Robbie.

Sean and Robbie got out, as did George Douglas and the male in the passenger seat.'

'Arite George' said Sean.
'Sean' said Douglas with a nod of the head. Everyone stood approximately ten yards from each other, sizing one another up. Robbie had no doubts that Douglas' mate was thinking *look at me the wrong way and I'll fucking smash ye.*
Robbie did his best to control the shaking in his legs, whilst thinking if this guy goes for it, hit him hard, hit him fast and move.
'What's on your mind George?'
'Thought we should discuss what happened to Starky.'

'Aye. What is there to discuss. Somebody fucking killed him. Unless you know who did it?'

'Well I can tell ye it wisnae any of my crew. Rumour has it, it was a couple of Scousers called Woody and Splinter.'

'How come none of my people have heard that?'

'Can't answer that, but I have it on good authority that it was because yer man Starky robbed the Scousers. Not a very smart move. Oh and they're not done. They are looking for the others that are involved, and if they find them, then they're gonna end up like Starky.'

'Starky done that without my knowledge, and he did it with his own guys. None of my lot are involved'.

'Maybe that's the case but I'd straighten it out with the Scousers before they come looking for you.'

'Worried about me George?'

Robbie could feel the tension rising. Douglas' mate never took his eyes off him for a second.

'Just trying to keep the peace. I don't want the Scousers getting their feet under the table in Dundee, coz they'll take over if that happens and that won't be good for either of us. I'm happy with our agreement. You run the Eastside and I run the Westside.'

'What if we pull our resources. To send the Scousers back home' said Sean.

That brought a smile to Douglas' face, 'that would suit you down to the ground now would it.'

'What's that supposed to mean?' asked Sean, who clearly took offence at what Douglas had said.

'Well. The way I see it is you're the one with the problem with the Scousers not me. It's your dealer they killed and it's not as if he couldn't have expected a reaction, robbing the Scousers. You get my people to help you get even with them. What do I get from it?'

'I wasn't suggesting it for that reason. I thought it would be best for both of us if we got rid of the Scousers. You said yourself, we don't want them getting their feet under the table, because regardless of what you think of me or anybody else, once that happens, we won't be able to stop them.'

'That may be true, but I'd rather take my chance they don't want a war than go to war with them foursomeone else's benefit.'

'Ok' said Sean who was clearly sizing Douglas up now. You could feel the tension in the air. All four of them were just staring at each other. Cammy and Hunter could only watch as they all waited to see who was going to make the first move. Who was going to be the first gunslinger to draw their weapon?

Sean broke the silence. 'So let me get this right. You asked for a meet just to tell me you weren't involved in Starky's murder?'

'I thought it best I tell you face to face. Plus I gave you the names of the people responsible.'

'So you're a fucking grass now.'

Douglas walked over to Sean. His expression may not have changed but Robbie could tell he was angry. Robbie thought, here we go and let the crowbar slip from the top of his arm to the bottom where he grabbed it, he was ready.

Douglas never took his eyes of Sean and saw him reach inside his jacket pockets. Douglas quickly closed the gap between them and punched Sean full force in the face. Robbie tried to stay focused on his man but was momentarily caught off guard by the sound made by Douglas' fist against Sean's face. It was a sickening thud, followed very quickly by the thud of Sean collapsing on his back hands still in his pockets.

People knew Douglas was a hard man, but Robbie couldn't recall anyone ever mentioning how fast he was. He could never recall seeing anyone knocking out Sean either, but then again Douglas was a big guy. Whilst this was happening Douglas' muscle produced the base of a pool cue from the rear of his jeans and was sprinting over to Robbie with the cue held up high in his right hand. As he brought the cue down at speed Robbie dodged the blow by diving to his right and in one deft move cracked the crowbar off the male's head. The male's body went rigid as soon as Robbie connected the crowbar with his head. He fell to the ground; he was out cold.

Robbie quickly turned to see where Douglas was, whilst he heard car doors opening. Cammy and Hunter had sprung out of the doors, like greyhounds from the traps. The doors being flung open caught Douglas' attention and he immediately shouted 'Now.'

Robbie saw Douglas turn around at look at the other van that was parked at the top of the Law Hill. The doors had flung open and four guys had jumped out. They all had weapons in their hands and were coming for Robbie, Cammy and Hunter.

Everyone was shouting and swearing, there were cracks of poles hitting pool cues and vice versa. Douglas swung for Hunter who was nearest him only to be caught by surprise by Hunter's skill in not only blocking the punch but also by the short sharp punch to the solar plexus which sent him backwards taking the wind right out of him.

Cammy was fighting with one of the guys that had jumped out of the van. He was throwing punches by the dozen some of which had hit the male in the face. Blood spurted out of the guys nose and from a large cut that had opened above his left eye. The left side of his face immediately began to swell. Cammy was giving this guy a right doing largely thanks to the knuckledusters he was using.

Robbie by this time had two males attacking him both of whom were trying to hit him with what he thought were pickaxe handles. He had studied Lau Gar Kung Fu when he was younger for five years and this was serving him well. He was managing to move around in such a way that only one of the males was able to get to him at one time. He blocked the first strike with the crowbar, and the second strike from the other male, but couldn't block the third strike from the first male. The pickaxe handle cracked against his left arm. The pain was instant and excruciating. His arm was broken and immediately went limp. As he swung to hit the male back with the crowbar, he saw Hunter kick the pick axe handle out of one of the males hands with his left foot before kicking him three or four times with his right leg to the guys left leg. The guy let out an enormous scream 'Aaaaaahhhhh he's broke my leg' as he clutched his leg.

Douglas was up by this point and had begun fighting with Cammy. Robbie was surprised at Cammy because he and Douglas were going toe to toe

punching one another when Hunter, ran over to help Cammy who was starting to come off worse in the exchange.
Douglas spotted Hunter running over and ran back to the van shouting 'You were bastard you're getting shot'. No one was sure if this was Douglas' excuse to avoid another fight with Hunter, or if he did have a gun. But they weren't staying to find out.

Everyone tried to get back to the car before Douglas pulled out a gun and started shooting. Robbie, Cammy and Hunter went to help Sean who was starting to come round by now. Hunter and Cammy threw Sean into the back seat. Cammy dived in the back seat too as Hunter jumped in the driver's side and Robbie the passenger side.

Robbie couldn't tell if Douglas even had a gun, but he wasn't taking any chances. The last thing he recalls seeing is several guys crawling, groaning on the ground, except the one with the broken leg who was still screaming. That is when it dawned on him. He never saw the fourth male from the van fight anyone, yet when he looked round, he was lying on the ground groaning. He looked at Hunter and thought it must have been him.

'Where did you learn to fight? That was awesome. I guess it was you who dealt with the fourth guy from the van?'
'Yeah. I am a martial arts instructor up north. I told Sean that.
That will be why he was so calm thought Robbie.
'That was fucking unbelievable I've never seen anybody kick George Douglas' arse'
'Where am I going by the way? Asked Hunter who was now the getaway driver and the coolest man on the planet. He did not appear fazed at all.

'At the bottom of this road turn left then take the first right, that'll take us onto Main Street' said Robbie as he sat with his head back holding his left arm which was throbbing.

'How's the arm?'
'It hurts like fuck.'
'Sean, Sean, Sean you arite?' said Robbie.

Sean, clearly still groggy tried to speak, but could only manage to mumble something inaudible.

Cammy was nursing his bruised face and hands.

'Sean, let us see yer face?' said Cammy.

Sean looked up and Cammy saw the full extent of his injuries.

'Fuck sake Sean, yer nose is broke, yer lips are bust and yer gonna have two keechers (black eyes) in the morning.'

'Tell ye what boys' said Sean a little clearer than before, 'I am gonna sort Douglas out once and for all. That bastard set us up. Cammy, do us a favour, never become a motivational speaker'. He may have been hurting but he still retained his sense of humour.

'Yeah well, they came off worse than we did' said Cammy.

'Take a right at the bottom of this road, keep going to the traffic lights, then take a left.'

'Ok.'

From there, Robbie spoke only to tell Hunter where to go to get them to Sean's flat. Everyone was nursing their injuries.

They parked up outside Sean's flat and went upstairs to the flat.

'Make yersels at home lad's, there's beer in the fridge. One of you guys will need to phone for a carry out, they'll no understand me just now.'

'Nae bother' said Hunter who immediately went to get a beer. 'Anyone want a beer?'

'Think I'll need to go to the hospital and get this arm plastered' said Robbie.

'I'll have a beer. Unless, do you want me to take ye up to the hospital? said Cammy.

'Wouldn't mind' replied Robbie.

Sean had gone to the bathroom to clean himself up and re-appeared ten minutes later. He had changed his top which had been covered in blood.

'What's next? Do you think he was telling the truth about Starky?' asked Cammy

'I do actually' said Sean.

'He gave us two names, didn't he?' said Robbie.

'Yeah should be able to find out if these two guys were involved. Even if they are Scousers' said Sean.

'Question is, did he tell us that to clear himself of any involvement or to get us to go war with the Scousers, or both?'

'Probably both' said Sean who was sitting on a recliner armchair with his head back looking up at the ceiling.

'So what do we do with that?' asked Robbie.

'We ask around. See if there is any truth in what he said. Then we take it from there'.

'Do ye want me to take you up to the hospital? said Cammy.

'Yeah. I'll check in with ye tomorrow Sean' said Robbie.

'Ok mate.'

Hunter finished his beer and said he would go with them to the hospital to save Cammy coming back for him.

'You gonna be ok?' said Hunter to Sean.

'Yeah, I'll be fine. Thanks for the help today. Any time you are needing extra money give me a shout, I can always do with someone with your skills' said Sean.

Not that Sean saw any of what went on, but he was not deaf or daft. He had heard the others speaking in the car and gathered that Hunter had saved them all from a severe beating.

Sean sat in the recliner and dozed off, having taken paracetamol for the pain. He woke several hours later but found the paracetamol had done nothing to ease the pain.

Meanwhile, Robbie had been informed that his arm was broken in two places but that he would need to return early this next morning to have it put in plaster. The breaks were both clean breaks, he was expected to be in plaster for 8-10 weeks, however. His immediate thought was that this left him vulnerable to attack from any of Douglas' gang. He figured by now Douglas will be rallying his troops, getting them prepared for war against Sean's squad.

He could not even contemplate what happens now between them and the Scousers. There was no way they could try to take them on, that would be suicide for Sean and his gang. But, this was assuming Douglas hadn't tried to trick them by saying the Scousers were responsible for Starky's death when it was his squad that did it, but Sean was a good judge when it came to assessing if people were lying to him and he thought, for once, Douglas was sincere.

Robbie phoned a taxi and went home for a few hours' sleep before he returned to have his arm plastered.

THURSDAY

After having his arm put in plaster Robbie got a taxi and went up to see how Sean was. He wondered if his best mate was feeling any better having taken a sledgehammer of a punch full force to the face. Robbie was amazed Sean even managed to get up afterwards.

Robbie was always mindful not to ask the taxi driver, a – if he had been busy today, b – what time he finished, c – if it was his own cab because it must be so annoying getting asked the same questions over and over every day. They arrived at Sean's flat within five minutes and although the taxi cost £7.40. Robbie gave the guy a tenner and told him to keep the change. Not that he was feeling flush he just hated public transport and the old guy driving the taxi was quite funny, ranting on about this that and everything.

He buzzed Sean's flat but got no response. As luck would have it, one of Sean's elderly neighbours was coming home as Robbie was about to leave.
  'Are you wanting a hand with your shopping dear?' asked Robbie seeing an opportunity to be friendly as well as getting himself in the building to check on his mate.
  'Oh that would be great son'
  'Give me the shopping and you get the door.'
  'Thanks son. Are you visiting somebody?'
  'Yeah, my mate Sean. Do you know him, lives in the top flat?'

'Yes I've met him before. A genuinely nice mannered boy, always asks how I am keeping.'

'That's him' said Robbie.

If there was one thing everyone would say about Sean is that he is very polite and respectful towards the older generations.

'Will you manage the shopping with your arm in plaster?'

'Yeah, I'll be fine. Is that you for the day? asked Robbie.

'That's my son. I'll get a cup of tea, biscuit and get my feet up and watch Columbo.'

'Sounds good to me.'

'I'm just here son' said the lady as she reached the second door on the ground floor.

'Will I just put your shopping here' asked Robbie as he placed the bags of shopping down at her feet?'

'That's great son thanks you.'

Robbie gave the woman a smile before turning to go up the stairs to Sean's flat.

Robbie knocked on the door, but there was no reply. He knocked again, louder this time, but again there was no reply. He phoned Sean but there was no reply to the phone call either.

That is strange thought Robbie. Sean usually answers his phone within seconds, I will try the door.

He tried the door and surprisingly found it unlocked. He walked into the flat shouting on Sean. He was still shouting on Sean when he entered the living room. Robbie did not find Sean in the living room or kitchen. That is strange he thought, unless he forgot to lock the door, or of course he could be in his bed, but at this time, (it was nearing two in the afternoon) I wouldn't have thought so. Robbie and Sean were good mates, but he did not want to go into his bedroom.

Just then he heard the toilet flush. Then he heard the door being unlocked and someone slowly coming down the stairs. He sat on the settee waiting to see if it was Sean. The living room opened very slowly and Sean trudged in.

'You look like shit mate' said Robbie in a typical Scottish manner which to anyone that is not Scottish sounds uncaring, but that isn't the case.

'Thanks mate. I feel like shit.'

'How's the face?'

'Sore. As you can see my nose is broke, I have two black eyes, my lips are better right enough, but my head is thumping.'

'Did you go to get checked out at the hospital?'

'Nah. They can't do anything for a broken nose anyway.'

'I'm thinking more of your head. Have you taken any paracetamol?'

'I took two last night, but it didn't really help, so I haven't taken any today. Well, as much as I hate the bastard, Douglas has a helluva punch. You know I've had loads of fights and been punched loads of times, but this was like being hit by a truck. I am still gonna get even though. He set us up.'

'You're right. He had a van full of guys there and he's not gonna help us take on the Scousers.'

'I'm beginning to wonder if the Scousers are involved at all. I think it could be him trying to deflect blame, so while we are planning on taking on the Scousers, he's planning to take over Dundee. But if he's smart, he'll wait until our squads depleted after fighting with the Scousers.'

'Nah mate. I actually thought he seemed genuine when he said it wasn't any of his crew.'

'Yeah, to be honest, I thought he was telling the truth too.'

'He's definitely gonna pay for setting us up, and for ruining my good looks' joked Sean.

'Calm down, calm down' said Robbie in his best Scouse accent, which made Sean burst out laughing only for him to say, 'don't make iz laugh, my face hurts.'

'I have had it confirmed that Starky did rob the Scousers, so he probably was killed by them.'

'Yeah, but Douglas is using that to set the two of us against each other. I mean you heard him. He gave us two names of guys that apparently did it. Since when we became grasses?'

'That's true.'

'Find out what you can about the guys Douglas says killed Starky. But you'll need to do it quietly because if it was them and they know you have been asking questions no doubt they'll come after you.'

'Maybe I should take Hunter with me. Man he can fight.'

'I gathered that although funny enough I didn't see it' said Sean with a little laugh.

'Well after Douglas hit you, Hunter went for him. Douglas threw a punch, but Hunter blocked it and punched him in the chest. Douglas decked it and could not get up for a bit. Then four guys got out of the other van that was parked there, and Hunter ended up kicking a pickaxe handle out of one of the guys hands before he kicked him a couple of times in the leg. The guy was screaming in agony. Then Hunter saw Douglas had got up and was fighting with Cammy. He was getting the better of Cammy when Hunter went to step in for him. Douglas crapped it, and said he was gonna get a gun and shoot Hunter, that's when we all split.'

'Bloody hell. Do you think he really had a gun?'

'Knowing Douglas. Yes. But we didn't stay to find out.'

'What happened to your arm?'

'Got hit by one of the guys wielding a pickaxe handle.'

'How long you gonna have the cast on for?'

'Anything between six to ten weeks, depending on how quickly it heals.'

'Ok.'

'Anyway I'm gonna get going. I will see what I can do regarding these two Scousers, Woody and Splinter. What you gonna do? I suggest you just chill for a couple of days.

'Yes mum' said Sean sarcastically.

'If you need anything give me a phone.'

'Cheers mate.'

Chapter 11

The investigation had seemed to stall over the next few days. There appeared to be no progress in any aspects of the investigation, it was extremely frustrating for Sharpe and his team.

MONDAY

It was the start of a new week and Marks parked his car in his usual space and walked into headquarters. 'Morning Mick, busy night?'
Mick Guild (the custody sgt) 'No pretty quiet. But there was one guy brought into custody that you might be interested in.'
'Who's that?'
'He's a Liverpudlian called Colin Crosby. Does the name mean anything to you?'
'No. Should it?'
'Probably not, but I think it'll be worth speaking to him' as he came out behind the public enquiry desk and lowered his voice. 'When I was doing the checks last night, he said he had information for CID, but that he would

only talk to the lead detective about it. When I asked what it was referring to, he said it was about a cop. Does not mean anything to me but it might to you. We checked him out on the intelligence systems but there is nothing of any significance on there, at least that I'm allowed access too.'

'That's brilliant. Thanks Mick. What's he in for?'

'Breach of the Peace and Police Assault but he's out on licence. If he offends within his probationary period, which runs until January next year, then he must return to prison to serve the remainder of his sentence, which if I recall correctly is two years. He was a bit drunk and was shouting off at a noisy music call. The cops warned him, but he told them where to go before he decided to fight with the cops. Doesn't look like much, but it took four officers to control him.'

'What time is he likely to be up at court?'

'Won't be before 11am. So you have got a couple of hours.'

'Great. Thanks for that Mick.'

Marks walked upstairs and popped his head into the CID offices looking to see if Sharpe was in yet, but there was no sign of him there, just a couple of detectives typing away at their computers.

He opened his office and switched the computer on, placed his briefcase beside his desk, opened his bottom drawer and got out his mug, sugar and his jar of decaf coffee. He could not drink the normal stuff anymore because it contained caffeine which exacerbated his anxiety. Even two cups a day of the normal stuff made a difference to him. He never brought in milk though, he would always pinch some of the DC's milk.

He went to the CID offices and asked if any of the nightshift detectives fancied a cup of tea or coffee. They both jumped at the chance of a coffee. Time was dragging on for them and they obviously felt the need for a jump start to get them through to the time when they would get some sleep. Marks made them coffee, albeit they got what was available in the kitchen and took it through to them. It was a simple gesture from the DCI but one that endeared him to them. None of the other senior officers would even contemplate offering to make them a cup of coffee.

They were both very grateful.

Sharpe appeared as Marks was returning to his office.

'Good morning Calum'

'Good morning Conor. Anything of note happen overnight?'

'Possibly. Get yourself a coffee and come into my office.'

Marks sat down and opened up all the applications needed for today.'

Sharpe came in, coffee in hand. 'What do we need to talk about?'

Marks gave him the information that he'd been given by Sgt Guild then proceeded to open up the intelligence database, having already noted down the Liverpudlian in custody's date of birth, address, criminal history number (which is unique to an individual) and apparent nickname.

Both he and Sharpe reviewed the situation together.

'Now according to the Scottish Intelligence Database (SID) Colin Crosby has several aliases, several dates of birth, numerous addresses and a tonne of intelligence entries relating to his involvement with drugs' said Marks. Sharpe was nodding in approval of what he was saying.

'Do you want to speak to him, whilst I review the intelligence database and contact Merseyside to see what they have on him?'

'Sounds good to me, but I'll give it a few minutes until one of the DS's come in and we'll bring him up to the interview rooms for a chat'.

'Ok. Well according to SID he's a small-time dealer for Paul MacDonald's drug gang. He sometimes goes by the nickname Splinter.'

'Weird nickname that.'

'I'm guessing he was either a fan of the Teenage Mutant Ninja Turtles or he was shite at football. (Nicknamed splinter coz he was always on the bench as a substitute)

'This will take some looking into because there's lots here' said Marks.

'Right. I will go and get someone to come down with me and bring him up. We will speak to him as soon as' said Sharpe. Sharpe got up and left whilst Marks continued to read each intelligence entry.

Sharpe saw that Lisa Bailey was in. 'Lisa, come with me.'

She put her handbag down by her desk and walked over to DCI Sharpe. He said something quietly to her and they walked off out the door that leads downstairs to the cell area. This will get them talking thought Bailey. Even the slightest indication that someone had a soft spot for someone in the police caused rumours. The police force is full of curious people, such is the nature of the job, that people always think people that spend longer than ten minutes together are having an affair. Sharpe checked in with the custody assistants.

'Good morning'
'Morning sir' said Ally (The male custodian)
'We're wanting to speak to Colin Crosby. We are taking him upstairs for a chat. How is he being
for you?'
'Fine. Has not been any bother at all. He did ask me to get someone from CID to speak to him
when they came in, but I haven't had a chance yet to phone up.'
'That's ok. We know how busy it can be down here' said Sharpe diplomatically.
'I'll go and get him.'
'That's ok. We will go and get him. Do not worry we'll sign the sheets to say where he is' said Sharpe.
'That'll be great. Thanks sir', said Ally as he handed him a set of jail keys. Sharpe looked through the peep hole to make sure he was awake and decent. After all, he did not want to open the cell door to find Crosby sitting on the toilet, lying naked or fondling himself.

Sharpe opened the door. As he did so Crosby sat up.
'You CID?'
'Yes, I'm Detective Chief Inspector Sharpe and this is my colleague Detective Sergeant Bailey. I believe you want to speak to us?'
'Yeah, can we go someplace else to speak?'
'Of course' said Sharpe, 'follow me.'
'What time is breakfast. I'm starving.'
'Don't worry I'll make sure they keep you a roll.'

Bailey signed the custody sheets to say where Crosby was and with who. There had been several incidents in years gone by where various officers from various departments had not signed the custody sheets to say where the person was. This resulted in everyone looking for a male who was sitting with officers in an interview room. Nothing causes panic in a police station more than a missing prisoner. On other occasions officers have taken clothing belonging to a prisoner, mostly to show to witnesses, to see if they can identify the person as being responsible for a crime. But they have failed to write that on the custody sheets that they have taken the item of clothing and why they've taken it. This has led to suspicion of theft by police. It has also prompted the quick-thinking criminal to claim his jacket which is now missing cost hundreds of pounds and not fifty quid.

They walked upstairs to an interview room where they closed the door and sat down.

'Now, what is so important that you wouldn't talk to any of my DC's, you need to talk to me?' asked Sharpe.
'Well. Let us just say you have an undercover cop that probably doesn't know the drug gang he has infiltrated know his real identity. What's more, I've got a fair idea I know who told the gang his real identity.'

'What's in it for me?' said Crosby.
'I'm sure we can work something out. How do you know this information? I mean no offence, but I can't see you being pally with the kind of people who would know the type of sensitive information' said Sharpe.
'No, fuck that. I want something in writing. I know how much this information is worth.'
'What do you want?'
'In relation to the police assault and breach of the peace.'
'Yeah.'
'But you're out on licence which means you need to return to prison to serve the remainder of your original sentence for aggravated assault, which is 2 years if I'm not mistaken.'
'Exactly. I can't go back to jail. Especially because my girlfriend just had my wee girl two weeks ago. My life has changed so much in two weeks and I can't go back to jail.'
'The problem we have is that you have already been put through our custody records on computer, so there's no way round that.'
'You either find a way round it or the undercover cop will end up getting murdered and if the media knew that you had a chance to save your buddy but didn't take it you'd get crucified by your bosses,' said a smug Crosby.

Sharpe knew Crosby was right. 'The best I can promise is to personally phone the magistrates in Liverpool and tell them you've been working with us. I'll also tell them if, and only if, our colleague is traced alive and well that you saved a police officers' life. How's that?'

'Would that get me out of here today?'

'I don't see why not.'

'That sounds like a deal to me' said Crosby.

'So, who is this cop and how do you know this information is genuine?'

'The cop, previously worked in Liverpool, it was years ago right enough, but I never forget a face. Especially when that face arrests your dad. When I saw him with MacDonald's Wirral gang a few weeks ago I did some digging. How I got the information isn't important, but the fact you haven't chucked me back in my cell tells me you know I'm right.'

'So who's the cop?'

'If I say, you can't let anybody know I gave you the name.'

'Don't worry about that. This isn't the first time we've done this.'

'Ok. The cops real name is Barry something...... I think. His undercover name is Garry Flynn.'

'You think he's called Barry?'

'Yeah. But he's told the gang his name is Garry Flynn and that he's the main man in the North East of Scotland.'

'Doesn't ring any bells with me' said Sharpe.

'Nor me sir' said Bailey.

'I'm telling ye. You guys will be able to find out his real name no bother.'

'How do you know all this?'

'I was in the room when MacDonald got the call. He was fucking raging. Started shouting and swearing saying he's gonna do this and that when he catches up with him. Lucky for him he hasn't been around since. But MacDonald has put a bounty on his head. If he's in Liverpool, he'll be lucky to get out of the city.'

'Did you hear who was on the phone?'

'No, but MacDonald said he owed the person big time and that he wished he could see his face when he realises who she really is.'

'She?' said both Sharpe and Bailey at the same time.

Crosby could tell by their voices they were surprised.

'When was the last time you saw Flynn?' asked Sharpe.

'About a week ago, in Aberdeen. He seemed alright, was chatting away to folk didn't appear to have any worries.'

Sharpe and Bailey looked at each other with concern etched on both their faces.

'Did he tell you where he was going or who he was meeting up with that day or the day after?'
'No.'
'What time did you last see him and who was he with?'

'The last time I saw him was about 11pm on Friday night. He was standing drinking with 4 Scousers, Steven Fowler – he's MacDonald's number two. John Paul Jackson, Paul Gowers and Neil Lawson in the Four Horsemen pub in Aberdeen. They've all booked a room for this Friday night in Aberdeen, according to Woody, when there's a big deal going down'.
'Who's Woody.'
'John Paul Jackson.'
'You never caught the name of the person who phoned?'
'No, but MacDonald at one point said, 'and he doesn't suspect a thing' and whoever he was speaking to must have said no because MacDonald said brilliant.'
'Is there anything else you want to tell us?'
'About what?'
'About who murdered the guy in the Hilltown.'
'Sorry, can't help you there, don't know anything about it.'
'Have you heard anyone talking about who did it or why he was killed?'
'Haven't heard anything, didn't even know someone had been murdered but if it was one of us Scousers that did it, I would've heard.'
'Just one last thing. Why are you up here?'
'I come up to see my cousin who stays here.'
'What's your cousin's name and where does he stay?'
'Tommy Campbell stays in Kirkton, but I don't know the address.'
'Do you know where the house is?'
'Yeah it's near Asda.'

'Ok. We'll put you back in your cell. You'll be called for court later this morning and in the meantime, we'll try and find Garry Flynn.'

Sharpe and Bailey escorted him back to his cell.

'Are you gonna make that phone call?' asked Crosby.
'Yeah I'll make it, can only promise to tell them you're helping us, in the end it's their decision.'
Crosby gave a little nod before the custody assistant locked the door.

'Something doesn't sit well with me about him' said Sharpe to Bailey.
'It does seem strange that you'd get someone whose been in that much bother with the police in the past giving us information like that' replied Bailey.
They reached the top of the stairs and Sharpe went to the left, towards Marks' office whilst Bailey went off to the right to go to her office.

Marks' door was open, and Sharpe knocked as he entered.
'You got a minute?'
'Of course. What's on your mind?'
'I've just spoken to the Scouser that's in custody Colin Crosby. He's been in bother with the police ever since he was a kid and yet he was willing to let us know that Barry Beaumont's identity has apparently been compromised. Not only that but that Paul MacDonald, the Scousers' main man has put a bounty on Beaumont's head. What's your thoughts?'
'Why would someone who's been in bother so much suddenly want to give the police information, especially when it comes to potentially saving a cops life? I mean you know these career criminals as well as I do, and they hate the police with a passion. I know he probably wants to avoid going back to jail but even still.'
'My thoughts exactly.'
'What's your gut telling you?'
'It's telling me something isn't right.'
'Did you ask him if he had any knowledge of Alan Stark's murder?'
'Yeah, said he didn't know anything?'
'Do you believe him?'

'I'm not sure, probably not. I mean, intelligence provides that he is a small-time dealer for MacDonald. MacDonald's right-hand man comes up to Dundee at the same time he does. No. He's got to know something.'

'I agree. Why don't you chase up forensics about the results of the stuff they found at Stark's flat?' said Marks.

'Yeah, I'll do that. Crosby's DNA will be on file, so we may get a hit. Thanks Conor.'

Chapter 12

Sharpe went to see Black next, to make sure he was fully aware of what was going on. He knocked at the door.

'Come in' said Black.
'Morning sir, have you got a minute, there's something I need to make you aware of?'
'Of course. What's on your mind?'
'I've just spoken to a male in custody called Colin Crosby. He said he has information that the drugs gang that a Gary Flynn has infiltrated know his real identity. He also said that Paul MacDonald, who as you know, runs one of the biggest drugs gangs in Liverpool, has put a bounty on Flynn's head. He also said that MacDonald knows the real identity of the cop after he received a phone call from a female who knows Flynn/Beaumont very well.'

'That's not good. Did he say when he last saw Beaumont?'
'Yes but it was last Thursday in a bar in Aberdeen. He's given us the names of people he was last seen with, so at least that's something. Plus he said they've booked a room in Aberdeen this Friday for a big deal that's going down.'
'I think we need to pull Beaumont out now. We can't take a chance that they know his real identity because the first chance they'll get they'll kill him.'

'I agree. But Beaumont's very experienced in undercover work, so it may be best to let him have the final say, after all he'll know if there's something not right.'

'Well, I think we should pull him out. It's too risky.'

'I'll speak to Kelly and get him to get Beaumont to call me ASAP and I'll speak to him see what he has to say about it.'

'Ok.'

Barry Beaumont was an experienced undercover cop. He'd had stints in the Drugs Squad before and gone undercover for months at a time and in all that time he learned the first rule of undercover work. Trust your instincts. Following this rule enabled him to successfully go undercover in various environments and cope with the pressures undercover work brought with it.

His first operation was as a clerk in a bookmaker where it was believed people were using the premises to deal drugs from. One staff member was suspected of being involved, although he didn't know to what extent. Having never bet a day in his life, he sought advice from the person he knew was as knowledgeable as anyone in a bookmaker – his brother Robbie.

Robbie had him up to speed within a couple of weeks. By which time he could calculate multiple winning bets in his head, knew what the Classic horse races were, where they were run, who had won them recently, what prices on football coupons were and how to advise people on the rules and regulations of betting.

It opened his eyes to a whole new world he never knew existed. The world of the gambler. This world consisted of everything to do with sport. No one ever talked politics, religion, music or even news, unless of course it was sports related. This was a very male dominated world, which ironically employed mostly women. However, Barry thought that it's probably because a large majority of the workers are women that it remained a male dominated world. He figured this because the women saw how gambling affected men's daily lives. How it consumed their lives, how it caused them to lie to their wives, girlfriends, boyfriends about how much they'd lost, and on occasions how angry the worried wives had been when they found their husband, yet again, in the bookmakers. What's more, was that most of the time it was the same men sitting in the same seats, spending their money.

Barry was undercover in the bookmakers for approximately 4 weeks. That isn't a long time, and it wasn't surprising to Barry because the drug dealing was so blatantly obvious to everyone that he was amazed it took so long for the bookmakers to make a complaint. In the end he arrested the assistant manager as well as the staff member they had initially suspected was involved. Numerous customers were caught in the sting however, they were used as witnesses against the bookmakers' staff. The two staff members eventually got sent to prison. The whole experience was an eye opener for Barry and one that stood him in good stead for years to come.

DS Black was in his office completing yet another paper exercise when he received a call from Barry Beaumont.

Beaumont spoke quickly and quietly. There was a big deal going down Friday night (Friday) between the Aberdonians and the Liverpudlians. The deal was worth about half a million pounds and there will be some major players at this meet. He believed that the gangs wouldn't be equipped with firearms but would confirm it whenever he could.

Black told him about the information they'd received that his identity had been compromised. Beaumont however told Black that he had only a few more days to last as Garry Flynn and he has invested a lot of time and effort in this operation. He said he would take his chances, after all they (Drug Gang) will be pre-occupied with the meeting and so he figures they'll not act until after the meeting by which time he will be out of danger having identified already himself as a cop.

He decided he would go into hiding to ensure that he wouldn't get caught out this close to the end of this operation by being seen entering a police station or being overheard on a phone call to someone in the police. If there was no contact, then they would be less inclined to think he was a cop.

The SCDEA still had access to MacDonald's phone thanks to the listening device Beaumont had managed to plant in his phone a little over a week ago. This is where the found out that there was a massive deal going down this Friday. But they required Beaumont to retain his cover until after the operation as they didn't know and wouldn't know the location of the operation until 2 hours before the meeting time. They did however know that the meeting was in Aberdeen.

As close as Beaumont had got to MacDonald and Fowler in the past year, he could not say where the deal was because only the top people in each gang knew this information.

The one thing that puzzled Beaumont was that up to yesterday, Paul MacDonald himself was supposed to be overseeing this deal, but for some reason decided to get his right-hand man to carry out the deal on his behalf. He didn't know why he pulled out, unless he suspected something, but then again surely, he would call the deal off, or something more urgent has come up.

Black knew the SCDEA would take the lead on this operation, but he needed to know roughly how many officers to provide them with in order to obtain the right people for the job. He knew he would need at least one PSU unit (Public Support Unit) if anything for a deterrent to those involved not to put up a fight.
The Public Support Unit, were ordinary cops who were trained in public disorder tactics. They were used primarily for big football matches, demonstrations and for angry prisoners. Even the criminals knew when the officers were carrying out this role, they weren't the same mild-mannered cops they met on the beat. The PSU were the cops the forces called for when they thought the shit was going to hit the fan.

Black also knew he would need firearms units to be stationed nearby just in case the gangs had firearms as well as uniform officers for detentions and or arrests.

There appeared to be very little he could control regarding this operation now and he didn't like it. Although he was very appreciative of

Beaumont's dedication and the information he provided, he needed know more.
A few moments later Black received a phone call from DCI Tom Kelly from the SCDEA. They spoke briefly about the operation tomorrow night, albeit both appreciated how flexible their plan had to be. Black said nothing about why Beaumont's identity may be compromised after all, he didn't know Kelly, he'd only ever spoke to him on the phone.

Black phoned Sharpe and Marks and updated them regarding the information Kelly had passed. However he had said in passing that he hadn't heard from Beaumont today (Friday). Being that the operation was today he thought that strange.

Sharpe had Bailey carry out the numerous checks on police computer systems for all the names they had that they suspected were of Liverpudlian drugs gang members. This took a while due to the volume of involvement everyone had with the police and the number of intelligence entries on these individuals. But Bailey knew this was a very worthwhile exercise because it allowed them to build a map linking the names to others they had and what their roles were inside the gang.

However, with each name they researched, the more they were finding out that this gang were utterly ruthless. If Beaumont's identity was compromised, they needed him out now.

Steven Fowler, Paul Wood, Colin Crosby, Neil Lawson, Jamie MacDonald, and John Paul Jackson were the names of the individuals they believed were involved in this drugs deal. All of them were prolific criminals. Between them they had amassed over 250 convictions ranging from shoplifting to attempted murder.

Fowler, MacDonald and Jackson all had previous convictions for attempted murder where they viciously assaulted two males by punching and kicking them as well as jumping on their heads.
Unfortunately one of the males had sustained such extensive injuries that he was left in a permanently vegetative state. Each of them had been

imprisoned for a few years each. The victim's family did try to lodge an appeal that the sentences were too light, but they were persuaded,

Crosby was considered a low-level drug dealer, but he had attempted to murder a man he thought had tried to make a pass it his girlfriend by stabbing him several times. Crosby had spent 6 years in prison before being freed early on the condition he doesn't re-offend, otherwise he would spend the unexpired portion of this sentence in jail. This was two years.

Wood and Lawson had a previous conviction of being caught in possession of a firearm. Both had served three years of a five-year sentence.

What made matters worse for the police was that all had a deep-seated hatred for the police. Beaumont really needed to be pulled out of this operation as soon as possible.

They didn't have any information about the vehicles they would be using, but they had decided to utilise the mobile cctv ANPR (auto number plate recognition). Hopefully, this would alert them to any vehicles that passed through the area that were registered in Liverpool.

TUESDAY

Sharpe had arrived at the office as usual about six thirty am. He had to assess how the investigation was going and what needed to be done today.

He phoned forensics bang on 9 o'clock.

'Forensics DC Miller.'
'Hi Pam, its Calum Sharpe here. Have you got the results from the Alan Stark murder scene yet?'
'Not yet, but we're expecting them today, although it will probably be later this morning.'
'Any chance of you letting me know as soon as possible? We've got somebody in custody on a separate matter, but I think he may be involved somehow.'

'Sure. No problem.'

'If for some reason you can't get me can you let DCI Marks know. His extension is 6976.'

'Ok sir.'

'Thanks' said Sharpe.

Sam Mason was carrying out a cctv review of the dvd's they had uplifted from the various businesses. He was on dvd number fifteen when he finally got a glimpse of Alan Stark walking past the entrance to a shop a few hundred yards from his home. He was on his own, but at least it was a starting place to try and piece together his last movements.

Mason and Wright had managed to narrow down Stark's time of death. Now all they were needing was descriptions of the murderers.

They now knew Stark's died between 2pm on Thursday 16th August and 0815 hours, Monday 20th August.

Marks contacted Louise Beaumont. She was pleased but incredibly surprised to hear from Marks.

'Hi, Louise its Conor Marks. How are you keeping?'

'I'm ok. Trying to keep myself busy to keep my mind off the fact I haven't heard from my husband for over a week.' She sounded pissed off but whether that was at the police or Barry he couldn't tell.

'Well, I'll try to put your mind at rest' said Marks, 'This is Barry's last day in his secondment, so he should be back home with you by the end of the week.'

'That's great Conor. Have you spoke to Barry today?'

'No, but the Detective Superintendent spoke to him yesterday.'

'Oh ok.'

He spoke to him only for a few seconds the other day and he said was ok and that he will be back home by Sunday at the latest.

'That's good. Did he say where he was?'

'No, but we think he's in Scotland, but I can't say any more than that. Have you got any other phone numbers for him since we last spoke?'

'No. Like I said he hasn't been in touch. Is he still in danger?'

'There's always an element of danger in the kind of work Barry carries out but Barry is very experienced, I'm sure if he felt that under threat, he would go to the nearest police station.'

'Yes, you're probably right. Thanks for phoning Conor. I appreciate you getting in touch.'

'No problem, I'll be in touch as soon as I have some news.'

'Thanks, bye, for now.'

Chapter 13

FRIDAY

Sharpe and his team hadn't been having the best of luck in the last few days. No one appeared to know anything about the murder, or at least that's the story they were sticking by. There were several names in the ledger found in Stark's safe, it was assessed that this information would be more beneficial if it were handed over to the force's drugs branch. After all, they were the ones in the know regarding the drugs scene and this ledger could be of great importance to them.
Black received a worrying phone call from Tom Kelly.
 'Hello Dave.'
 'Hello.'
 'It's Tom Kelly here. The deal is taken place later today at Clarks Carpets Milligan Estate at 7pm. Nobody will have firearms and we suspect there will be about 10-12 people involved. However we have a problem' said Kelly.
 'What's that?'
 'I haven't heard from Beaumont since about seven o'clock last night, and in the year, he's been undercover with us, he's never not been in contact the day of the operation.'

Black said he would task officers to carry out what enquiry can be done from Dundee. He admitted to Kelly he was fearful that Beaumont could have come to harm. He was cursing himself. He should've ordered him out of the operation. Both he and Kelly suspected the Liverpudlians were behind Beaumont's disappearance. Black said he would ensure the necessary paperwork is completed as soon as possible in order to increase their chances of having Beaumont's phone located.

Kelly knew this was a big operation and was one that they were in touching distance of finishing with the prospect of a good result, nonetheless he had the courtesy to ask Black if he wouldn't mind if they continue with the operation. Not that the operation would be put off, he simply wanted it on record, should something happen, that DS Black was board. Black knew this and said to go ahead otherwise all of Beaumont's hard work will all have been for nothing. Kelly thanked him for making that decision and said he would be in touch as soon as they had concluded the operation.

Black contacted Sharpe in the first instance and told him to have Sharma and Munro report to him immediately. If, for some reason they weren't available, he was to contact Black.
Munro appeared first and was immediately tasked with tracing Beaumont's phone.

Meanwhile Marks was getting ready to leave when Sharpe knocked on his door. Once he updated him regarding Beaumont's latest disappearance Marks took his jacket off, sat back down and began co-ordinating with Black and Sharpe what was needing done.

Munro had the paperwork done within minutes. All that was required was changes to the dates and slight change of circumstances. However, it now had to be carried out through the control room as their intelligence unit had finished for the day. The enquiry was passed to Sgt Martin in the control room due to its sensitive nature.

He said he would contact DCI Marks when he had an answer to the enquiry.
Black could do no more from where he was. He had to put his faith in Kelly and his colleagues at the SCDEA that they were fully prepared to deal with this situation. But Black made sure everyone he had organised to be ready should they be required, was ready.

The warehouse was massive. There were offices to the left of the front door entrance and toilets slightly to the right of these. Further to the right were large steel shelving units, obviously in place for the carpets. Situated between the large steel shelving units and the toilets was a large sliding door. This was where the deliveries were taken in.

The warehouse had no electricity in it as it had been closed for business for almost a year. This was noticeable by the damp, musky smell and the fact the place was covered in bird crap.

This could prove to be a problem for Kelly and his colleagues because although the microphones were strong enough to pick up a whisper at the other side of the warehouse, the darkness meant their video cameras wouldn't be good enough to pick out who said what. They couldn't risk getting any closer without being seen. The warehouse was empty and there was literally nowhere to hide bar the offices or the toilets, and they couldn't risk hiding in the toilets for obvious reasons.

It was a tense wait for Black. He was no stranger to high pressure situations, but it was a strange experience for him sitting at a computer whilst others tried to resolve the situation. He felt helpless but he had faith in his colleagues.

They sat poised to strike when the officer on overwatch let Kelly and his team know that a car full of people was approaching the rear delivery door.

It was about five to seven when the car pulled up outside. The front seat passenger got out and walked over to the sliding door. The guy was huge. At least 6'6 and extremely muscular. The officer on overwatch duty, was watching from a disused office about 100 yards away through a pair of binoculars. He thought this guy is going to take some holding back if he kicks off. The giant walked over to the door, which was usually locked, but thanks to the local youths vandalising it, was now unlocked. He slid the huge door open with ease and the car drove into the warehouse. The car drove to the far end of the warehouse before settling close to the offices, facing the entrance/exit ready for a quick getaway.

Kelly was thankful that he had decided not to let his officers try and hide in the shadows because the cars headlights would've exposed them and scuppered any chances of the deal being done and them getting an arrest. It would also have caused months of undercover work to have been wasted.

The giant remained at the door whilst looking out for any other vehicles. Although the officers knew the deal involved people from Aberdeen and Liverpool, they believed this man mountain was one of the Aberdonian gang. He was looking for the Scousers. The cops sitting in the two vans situated around the side of the warehouse remained ready to go.

They didn't have to wait long before a second vehicle arrived. The vehicle was driven through the gate entrance. The driver slowed down and raised his right hand from the steering wheel to acknowledge the big guy at the door, who gave them the thumbs up. The car was then driven into the warehouse where it stopped a few feet from the bumper of the car already parked there. Both vehicles kept their headlights on. This didn't help Kelly's officer filming the deal because it was too bright. The video camera couldn't focus properly and was proving to be a waste of time at least while the car headlights stayed on.

The doors of both vehicles opened, and five people got out of the first vehicle and five people got out of the second. One of the people that got out of the second vehicle was a tall male, who appeared to have his right hand bandaged. The last person to get out of the first vehicle was very smartly dressed in a suit, with a crisp white shirt, no tie and well-polished shoes.

The male from the second vehicle whose hand was bandaged walked over to the smartly dressed male. As he approached him, he stretched out his hand. 'Steven Fowler, how you doing?'

The smartly dressed male took this opportunity to shake his hand. 'Johnny Collins. Pleased to meet you Mr Fowler. Shall we get down to business?'
'Yeah, sure. Have you got what I asked for?'
'Of course. I wouldn't want you to have a wasted journey.'
'Good. Well let's see the stuff.'
'Follow me' said Collins as he walked off to the back of the car.
Fowler followed. Collins opened the boot before opening a large sports bag which revealed what Fowler had travelled from Liverpool for.

Fowler signalled to one of his men who reached into the rear seat of the car. He brought out a bag and walked over to Fowler who said nothing. The male seemed to know his duties, as if they had practised what to do on the day. He showed Collins the contents of the bag which brought a smile to Collins' face.

'Nice doing business with you' said Collins as he took the bag from the male, who in turn took the bag out of the boot and walked off towards their car.

'Same again next month?' asked Fowler.

'Sure. I'll be in touch' said Collins.

That was that.

As all parties were walking to their cars the sound of their footsteps was quickly drowned out by a host of voices shouting 'Police, stay where you are' as Kelly and his colleagues made their presence known by sprinting towards them. With every officer shouting and the echoes of their shouts bouncing around the warehouse, it sounded like an army of cops were there. The drivers got in the cars and started the ignitions, but there were so many people running about all over the place the drivers couldn't go, at least not without the risk of knocking over some of their own gangs.

Kelly appeared to have thought of everything. Officers ran towards the drivers of the cars, whilst others ran towards the nearest man to them. The speed at which the cops moved was impressive and it was this speed coupled with the element of surprise that allowed them to capture everyone involved.

Not that the gangs made it easy for the police. One male ran outside but was pursued by a young cop who produced a rugby tackle that wouldn't have looked out of place in a six nations rugby match. Two of the gang tried to run off. But they simply ran into the officers that had been hiding themselves away in the two vans parked at the side of the premises ready to go when they got the shout. Whilst the giant who had been watching the door didn't even try to run.

Kelly considered it to be a highly successful operation but for one thing. There was no Barry Beaumont involvement in this operation. Why? No one knew where he was. Did the Liverpudlians know his real identity? If they did, how did they know? As a result of the operation, ten people were arrested. Over 10 kilos of drugs were recovered, including Cocaine, Heroin and Marijuana, as well as a large amount of cash, which they would seize from the drugs gangs. This was a major blow to the drugs gangs, because they had captured one of Liverpool's top drug dealers and some of Aberdeen's biggest drug dealers. They had also succeeded in taking their half a million pounds from them. Although they would have to apply to the courts to seize the money, there was no doubt a sheriff would approve the confiscation request.

It had been two hours since the operation was supposed to have been executed when he received a call from DCI Kelly. Everything went very well. Kelly informed him that the joint operation between the SCDEA and Police Scotland had resulted in the arrest of ten people involved in the drug deal. Five people from Aberdeen and five from Liverpool, including Steven Fowler who was reputed to be the second in command of the Liverpool gang. They recovered the drugs and the money but there were no firearms found.

Kelly also confirmed that Beaumont had failed to show up tonight. Beaumont had been an excellent addition to their team. He was a hard worker, got on with everybody and was particularly good at his job. It had already been arranged that once all the paperwork was done and dusted, he was to return to Dundee. Although Kelly told Black he would welcome him back into the SCDEA without hesitation should he want to return. Black thanked him for that but couldn't help fearing the worst. Black had told Beaumont that his identity had most probably been compromised, but he stayed undercover and now no-one knows where he is.
Black told Kelly that he wished he had instructed him to come out of the operation. This could be a decision he lives to regret. Kelly however said that in his opinion, of what he knows about Beaumont, there was no way anyone would pull him out of this operation. Kelly was adamant something had happened to Beaumont, he was hoping he was wrong, but he didn't think so.

Chapter 14

SATURDAY

They still hadn't heard from Beaumont. Everyone was now fearing the worst.

Sharpe and his team were about to get the change of luck they were needing. Within an hour of phoning forensics DC Miller was back on the phone. She had the results of the fingerprint lifts, including the one lifted from the bag of drugs that were found in the safe, the fingerprint lifted from the knife block where they believed the murder weapon was taken from. They also had DNA from blood splattered on the hall wall that didn't belong to the victim, and they also had a DNA hit from the blood that they uplifted from the handrail in the close.

The fingerprint found on the bag of Cocaine found in Stark's safe was found to belong to none other than Colin Crosby. When Sharpe heard this, he thought your cheeky wee shite! You gave us information, not to save a cop, but to have a chance of saving your own.

The fingerprint found on the knife block came back as belonging to Steven Fowler.

The blood spatter found in the hall of Stark's flat belonged to Crosby.

The blood found on the handrail in Stark's close came back as Stark's and Crosby.

'We still have a partial footprint that we haven't identified as anyone's so if you get hold of a suspect, remember and take their shoes' said Miller.

Sharpe couldn't contain his delight. As soon as he came off the phone, he commanded everyone's attention.

'Listen up folks. That was forensics on the phone we've got a fingerprint hit and a DNA hit in relation to Starks' murder. The fingerprint found on the knife block belongs to Steven Fowler. The name probably doesn't mean anything to anyone up here, but Fowler is one of Liverpool's top drug dealers. Plus, he was arrested in Aberdeen last night as part of a drugs operation. So it looks like he took the knife from the knife block in Stark's kitchen therefore he's probably the one that slashed and stabbed him. The blood found on the wall in the hall that didn't belong to Stark belonged to Colin Crosby.'

'That lying little git' said Bailey.

'I know and he said he didn't even know anyone had been murdered.'

'That's why he gave us information, to see if we can get him released and he'd no doubt flee the country' said Bailey.

'Do you want to be the one that detains him for murder?'

'I'd loved that.'

'Then go get him. Take DS Budd with you' said Sharpe.

'Oh and take his trainers. There's still a partial footprint we have to identify who it belongs to.'

At this point Sharpe picked up the phone and phoned his counterpart in Aberdeen. He needed to make sure that the trainers of all the Liverpudlians were taken for comparison against the partial footprint found in blood in Stark's flat.

Sharpe went to tell Marks the good news. Marks was understandably happy. They had great evidence against two people for the murder of Alan Stark in Steven Fowler and Colin Crosby. They also had Crosby for drugs offences too.

They also had to review cctv near to Starks' flat to see if they could place Crosby or Fowler in the area. With a little bit of luck, they would capture them on cctv and that would provide them with the clothing they were wearing at the time of the murder. They were being greedy now but if they could get that clothing too, that'd be perfect.

Sharpe contacted Crichton and Milne and gave them the good news. He also gave them a description of what Steven Fowler and Colin Crosby were currently wearing. Whilst it's unlikely they were wearing the same clothes when they killed Stark you never know. They now had the images of both males too.

Mid-morning and the feeling inside police headquarters were one of delight. You could sense the good feeling in the place as soon as you walked through the door and quite right too. Not only have the officers identified two people for the recent murder. They captured some of Britain's biggest drug dealers and managed to seize their drugs, and hundreds of thousands of pounds in drug money.

Everyone connected with the police were sure to have a good Saturday night. Well not everyone.......
Meanwhile Robbie and Sean were using their contacts in the police to try and find out if there were any Liverpudlians known to police that go by the nicknames Woody or Splinter. To their amazement, they were both told by their contacts that several Liverpudlians had been arrested for drug dealing. Robbie finished his call and said to Sean 'Fucking unbelievable. The cops busted a load of guys trying to carry out a big deal in Aberdeen and five of them are Scousers and get this, one of the guys has the nickname Woody. Apparently because he's a dead ringer for that American actor Woody Harrelson, you know him that was in Natural Born Killers.'

'I fucking love that film' said Sean.

'It was ok, although Juliette Lewis was pretty hot in it. Anyway, as I was saying one of the guys is called Woody. Apparently, his real name is John Paul Jackson' said Robbie.

'I've also just had a text from a mate. He said that they (police) have also arrested a guy called Colin Crosby, who goes by the nickname Splinter for Starky's murder. Not only that but they've got enough to charge another guy Fowler with the murder as well.'

'Bloody hell, so is that two for Starky's murder?' asked Sean.

'Yeah two. Crosby aka Splinter and some guy Steven Fowler.'

'Douglas said one of the guys that killed Starky was called Woody, did he not?'

'Yeah. Well he's got one guy right and a guy nicknamed Woody got arrested for dealing'

'So all things considered his information was pretty good' said Robbie.

'We'll get even for Starky, might take time, but we'll get even for him.'

Robbie said nothing to Sean, but he was thinking if Starky hadn't tanned the Scousers flat, battered the two guys in there and stole their gear and their money, they wouldn't be in this predicament.

Sean disappeared into the kitchen and came out with two tins of Stella for them.

'Let's drink to Starky', as they both held their beers up 'here's to you, you mad bastard, but ye were our mad bastard. Starky.'

They both said Starky, banged the cans together and started drinking their beers.

'What happened to the two guys Starky and his mates beat up?' asked Sean.

'I heard that one of them is still in hospital and the other guy got out after a few days. Apparently, he went straight back to Liverpool' said Robbie.

'Did we ever find out who was with Starky?'

'Yeah, well rumour has it, it was the King twins, Davie and Darren and John Smith'.

'What the dancer, Begbie and simple Smithy?'

'Yeah, that's what I heard anyway.'

'I thought you said it was a guy called Goofy or something that was involved?'

'Yeah, that's what I heard initially, but it turns out he had a pile of money coz he stole some old dears handbag. He was saying he helped rob a drug dealer to get away from the fact he mugged a granny.'

'The thieving shite. Hope he gets done over. That's no right mugging a pensioner. Dunno if I believe that Dancer was involved though. John Smith probably, because although he's simple, he'd fight a fucking gorilla if ye offered him twenty quid, and Begbie, he lives up to his nickname does he.'

'Begbie, fuck aye. In fact he makes original Begbie look like a choirboy. Strange innit?'

'What is?'

'How you can have twins that are so different. I mean Begbie. Fucking off the charts psycho and yet dancer – well, he's a lover not a fighter, is he?'

'I guess so. I'm surprised the Scousers haven't caught up with them.'

'Yeah, but then again, quite a few of them got nicked over the weekend did they.'
'I suppose. Can't see them forgetting though.'
'No me neither.'
'Anymore?' asked Robbie as he held his empty tin of Stella up.
'Aye, in the fridge, bring me in one as well mate.'

Robbie and Sean opened another tin of beer and chatted away all night having beer after beer until they both fell asleep where they were.

Chapter 15

SUNDAY

Sunday morning, in Dundee and the fog hadn't lifted. The grass was soaking wet and the park was becoming busier as more dog walkers started to appear. Everyone in the park appeared to be easing into their Sunday morning except for the two men putting up football nets for the kids' football later in the morning.

'Hector, Hector' shouted one dog walker trying to recall his dog as it buried its head amongst several black bin bags which had been dumped beside a dog waste bin. 'Hector, Hector come' shouted the man once more, but to no avail. Whatever Hector was smelling had grabbed his attention and it seemed as if nothing was going to tear him away from these bags.

'Hector, Hector come here' shouted the man, who was quite clearly getting irritated by his dog's lack of obedience. 'Hector come' said the man who by now was marching across to the dog. The dog popped his head up, tail wagging furiously, picked up something in its mouth and ran over to the man. The man was getting ready to put the dog back on the lead when he saw that Hector appeared to have a strange object in his mouth. As Hector reached him the man saw that Hector had in his mouth a human hand.

He looked round and saw the men putting the nets up and shouted 'Help, help'. The two men ran over whilst the man stood there shaking. 'Are you okay?' shouted one of the men.

'It's my dog' said the man pointing to Hector who was lying down licking this human hand, 'he's got a hand'.

'Bloody hell so he has', said one of the men in disbelief.
The other man went over to Hector, who let him pick the hand up. Hector wagging his tail, getting set, getting ready to fetch what he thought was a toy.

The man who now had the hand asked to speak to his mate and asked him to phone the police whilst he asked the dog walker if he could go and sit on one of the benches until police arrived. His friend was leading the dog walker, who by now had Hector on the lead. One of the men asked Hector's owner where the dog found the hand.

'Over there, in the black bags' said the man.

'Ok. 'I'll go and stand guard near the bags so that no one, or no other dogs disturb the bags,' and off he went, stopping about 20 yards from the bags, with the hand now on the grass beside his feet.

The dog owner, who was traumatised, began walking towards a park bench. They could hear the sirens already and within a minute a police car came screeching up to the car park. Two male officers got out of the car and approached the man who now had a human hand at his feet.

'Are you the gentleman that phoned?' asked one of the officers.

'No it was my mate' as he pointed towards the park bench. 'I've come over here to protect the scene.'

'That's brilliant thanks. How did you know to do that?' said the officer.

'I'm at Tulliallan (Scottish Police College) just now on my initial training' said the man.

'Well, well done' said the officer as he began taking a pair of blue latex gloves out of his jacket.

He put them on before saying 'thanks for your efforts, if you go towards my colleague, he'll take a statement when he can, and I'll protect the scene until SOCO get here.' He picked up the hand which by now had been licked and nibbled by Hector the dog, before walking over to the bin and placing the hand on the ground. He didn't get too close because he didn't want to disturb the scene.

Sharpe was contacted and immediately advised the officers on scene to cordon off the whole football area of the park.

DS Budd was on duty and was appointed the Crime Scene Manager. He attended the locus along with DC Sam Mason who had recently moved to the Scenes of Crime Team permanently.

Marks had the luxury of a lie in which was a rare event. Susan thought it best to let him sleep, despite meaning he would miss his 6am tablet. As she kept reminding him, he had to listen to his body now, and being that he slept through his alarm.

It was just after nine when he awoke. He had ambled his way downstairs and into the conservatory and was finishing his coffee when the phone rang. It was his works mobile that was ringing, this wasn't good. No one phoned Marks to give him good news.

'Hello'
'Hello Conor, its Calum.'
'Let me guess, bad news?' said Marks hoping he was wrong.
'Well we can't say for certain, but it looks like it. A man out walking his dog this morning found a human hand that was in a black bag beside a bin. Although we've only found a hand at the minute there are three black bags beside this bin, and it's suspected there could be other body parts in the other bags. What we do know, is that when the man's dog ripped open the bag a gym membership card fell out of the bag in the name of Barry Beaumont. So it's not looking good.'
'No it doesn't.'
'I'm just letting you know because if it turns out to be Beaumont right enough, then I figured you'd want to go round and speak to his wife' continued Sharpe.
'You're right, I think I know them as well as anybody and I think it makes sense I do it.'
'Ok. Well SOCO are on their way to the scene and I'm on the way there now. I'll let you know what I find.'
'Thanks Calum.'

SOCO were putting their paper suits on when Sharpe arrived.
'Good morning guys' said Sharpe.
'Good morning' came the reply.

'Have you been here long?'

'No, just a couple of minutes' said Budd.

'Have you got a suit for me to put on? Asked Sharpe.

'Yeah' said Mason as he reached into the van and pulled a paper suit from a drawer before handing it to Sharpe.

'Thanks. What have you been told?'

'Just that a hand has been found in a black bag and that there are other bags there. So the thought is that there could be other body parts there. So we'll treat it as if there are other body parts there, and if there isn't well at least we've done it right, from the start' replied Budd.

'My thoughts exactly' replied Sharpe.

They were almost fully suited up when a sergeant in uniform came up to them and asked Sharpe if he wanted the man and his dog conveyed to police headquarters for a statement to be taken.
Sharpe, however, asked how the man was. The sergeant said his officers told him that the man was quite badly shaken up. Sharpe informed the sergeant to convey him and his dog home. After all it would have been a frightening ordeal for the man and if they had his details and statements from the other men there, they could always obtain a statement from him later.

At that, the sergeant walked off towards the men sitting on the bench.

Sharpe, Budd and Mason checked they had all the cameras, video cameras, and other equipment they were needing.
They walked over to the bin, taking their time to look at the grass to see if there were any signs of blood to indicate where the bags had been carried from, but they couldn't see any.

'Good morning' they all said to the constable in uniform who had been tasked with standing guard at the scene, albeit he was approximately 20 yards away from the bin.
Not knowing either of the three's rank he said 'Morning sirs.'

They each acknowledged the uniformed officer, signed the Crime Scene Log and logged the time they entered the scene.

Mason was already taking pictures of exactly where everything was. They noticed there was blood seeping from the bag that had been ripped open. They had brought a plastic crate to place the ripped bag in so that the none of its contents were lost.

Every bag SOCO took was going to be opened in the mortuary as per normal procedure under the circumstances. Only then would they know the contents of each bag. Everything is photographed and laid out before the police and the pathologist begin putting the body parts together.

Once they had finished up in the park, they made their way to the police mortuary. Once Sharpe, Budd, Mason, Dr Dempster and her faithful assistant were ready they opened the first bag.

This first bag to be opened was the ripped bag. This bag contained the right hand and right leg of a man. Also found within the bag were numerous cards, bank cards, store cards, and membership cards to various places all in the name of Barry Beaumont.

They opened the second bag. This contained the left leg and left hand. Nothing else of any note was found in this bag.

The third and final bag was the heaviest bag of all. This bag contained the torso, but they were still missing the persons arms and head. The only clues to the identity of the victim was the cards in Beaumont's name. There were no tattoos or scars on the body parts recovered.

When Sharpe returned to the office, he went to speak to Marks. He updated him on their find and they both agreed that Louise should be told about what they had discovered already before the press gets wind of this story.

Marks made sure he was aware of all the latest updates regarding the enquiry before he left headquarters to speak to Louise. He informed Sharpe where he was going and asked him to update him with any new information. The journey to Beaumont's house was only a twenty-minute drive, but it felt a lot longer. Although Marks had passed numerous death messages before, he never knew what the reaction of the family would be. Whilst some people broke down others appear to take the news quite well, he always put this down to news not sinking in. But he had a feeling that due to their previous meeting, where he told Louise Beaumont that they believed her husband was in danger, she would blame them for her husband's murder.

However, Marks would be lying if he said he didn't, at this point, partly blame the decision to keep Beaumont undercover for this too.

He parked his car in front of the Beaumont's drive and began walking up the path to the door when he caught a glimpse of Louise Beaumont at the living room window. By the time he reached the door she had opened the door.

'He's dead, isn't he?'
'We'll speak inside if that's ok' said Marks as he ushered her into her living room.
'Conor' she said sternly 'just tell me. Is he dead?'

Marks sat down and said 'Louise a member of the public found a bag containing human body parts, now at this moment in time we do not know who this person is, but we did find bank cards, store cards and a gym membership all in Barry's name within the bags.'
'So somebody's murdered him and cut him up' said a stunned Louise.
'It may not be him, but I thought I'd better let you know what we know.'
'Murdered' said Louise in disbelief.
Louise's disbelief quickly turned to anger as she began shouting and screaming at Marks 'YOU ALL KNEW HE WAS IN DANGER AND YET YOU LEFT HIM UNDERCOVER, HE SHOULD HAVE BEEN PULLED OUT THEN THIS WOULDN'T HAVE HAPPENED. YOU KILLED HIM. THIS IS ON YOU. GET OUT GET OUT' as she began pushing Marks out of the house.

Marks didn't try to reason with her. How could he. She's just been informed her husband has likely to have been found cut up into pieces days after police had been at her house saying they believe her husband's in danger. No-one could blame Louise for reacting this way.

Marks got up and left. He didn't try to say anything. He got in his car and drove back to headquarters.

The drive back to headquarters seemed to take forever. Never has Marks recalled every second of a journey. He kept thinking about what Louise had said YOU KILLED HIM. THIS IS ON YOU.
Marks was an experienced cop, but no amount of experience prepares you for someone blaming you for the death of a loved one.
Marks didn't blame Louise for saying what she said. Anyone in her shoes would probably think the same way. When Marks got out of the car he shuffled up to his office. He didn't look up, speak to or even acknowledge anyone. Although it was too early to say for definite if they (Police) as an organisation were fully or partly to blame, they first had to establish who the victim was, who killed him and why. It may have nothing to do with his undercover work, but it was a big coincidence if it wasn't. Marks sat in his office, switched his computer on and stared at the screen whilst loaded up.

There was a knock at the door and then the door opened. It was Dave Black.

'How did it go?'
'She blames us. She said we should've pulled him out and she could be right you know.'
'Yes, I know. But you just said it yourself.... could be....
'The thing is we'll never know if us leaving him under cover contributed to his death or not. I mean if it is him, and if he was killed because of his undercover work, then we'll never know if it still would've happened if we'd pulled him out.'
'I'm not disputing there are lessons to be learnt here but listen to what you've just said. There's a lot of ifs and maybes at the minute. Plus I know it's no consolation, but we did give him the choice. We told him he should pull out, he chose to stay in. Besides whom says it has anything to do with his undercover work. I mean it's highly likely it was, but what if it wasn't.

What if it was a pissed off husband of the wife, he's having an affair with. Or a pissed off wife of a husband he's having an affair with' said Black.

'Yeah you could be right. He did say to Louise he'd be gone three nights but only booked to stay at the hotel for two.'

'Maybe because the third night he had plans with someone.'

'Apparently nobody saw him after 7pm on the Thursday. So could it be that he met someone, planned or not and the reason he wasn't seen afterwards was because he was killed that night' said Marks.

'Yeah that's possible, but why dump the body in Dundee?'

'Unless he came back to Dundee for some reason.'

'Anything's possible. I mean it's only an hour up the road.'

'I'll contact Kelly and confirm when he was last seen by his team and see if he gave them any indication if he was going to meet anyone, or where he was going?'

'Ok. I'll let you and Sharpe sort out the enquiry, just keep posted.'

'Of course.'

Black returned to his office whilst Marks phoned Kelly to get the answers to his questions.

Kelly had spoken to his team and told Marks that they, as well as, Beaumont stayed at the Premier Inn hotel on the waterfront on Thursday night. They had all planned to stay there Friday night due to the late finish they anticipated may happen. But no-one remembers seeing Beaumont after tea, on the Thursday which they finished at around 7pm. One officer said he recalls Beaumont saying he had to nip home to see his wife because he hadn't seen her for a couple of days but that he'd be back up to meet them at the hotel mid-morning. When he didn't appear, they thought he may have been with the Scousers and unable to get away from whatever they were doing at the time.

As the day wore on, they started to become concerned and that's when Kelly phoned DS Black.

Marks updated his computer file he had created and kept updating in order to assist him in recalling what he said and to whom he said it. Marks had noticed incredibly early on in his Parkinson's diagnosis that he struggled to retain information and so he started keeping records to remind himself of things.

Once he had updated his file, he phoned Black. Ordinarily he would have walked to his office, but his knees were throbbing, he couldn't explain it, he just accepting it and got on with his work.

'I'll go back around tomorrow see what I can find out. By then we should know more about the murder' said Marks.
'If you think it'll help get Sharpe to go around instead of you' replied Black.
'No. I'll go, but I'll phone her first.'
'The SCDEA arrested five Liverpudlians as part of the big drugs deal didn't, they?' asked Black.
'Yeah, but of course they could've killed him before the drug deal. Or there could be more Scousers in Aberdeen.'
'It seems highly unlikely that they'd bring up different people to deal with Beaumont and the deal. Surely the five of them that were there for the deal would've dealt with Beaumont if they had to' said Black.
'That's true.'
'Plus they were only getting two hours' notice where and when the deal was happening. They were arrested during the deal, so they would have had to kill him, cut up the body, and dispose of the body beforehand. This would mean driving all the way down to Dundee, an area that thy may not know too well, and find a quiet area to dump the bags.'
'Yes, when you think about it, it's highly unlikely to have been them is it?'
'I think we're looking for someone he met up with that night. I'll ask Louise if she recalls Barry saying he would be returning Thursday night. I'm sure she would have mentioned it.'
'I'm sure she would have. You would imagine it would take some time to cut a person up and put the body parts into bags. At least a couple of hours.'
'That's assuming you knew what you were doing and had the right tools for the job. I'm thinking, there's no doubt the SCDEA will have seized their vehicle for a full search. I'll ask them if there are any traces of blood within. If there isn't then it wasn't them because there's no way you would be able to transport a body in bin bags and not leave some blood in the car.'

'Good thinking Conor. Keep me updated.'

Marks, Sharpe and his team pressed on with their enquiries.
Marks phoned Kelly. He asked him if they had found blood in any of the two vehicles they had searched as a result of the drugs bust. Unfortunately neither vehicle was found to contain any traces of blood. Having taken into account the timescales involved in Beaumont's disappearance. The drug bust, the discovery of his body parts, and the fact that no blood was found in the Liverpudlians car means that it would have been impossible, at least for these five Scousers, to have murdered Barry Beaumont.
Sharpe and Marks were relieved and worried at the same time. If, as now thought, the Scousers hadn't killed Beaumont, then who did. The answer must surely be in connection with Beaumont's personal life. The big worry for them, was that it takes an extremely depraved character to dismember a body. In both Sharpe and Marks' experience even the most psychotic killers find it too gruesome to dismember a body.

MONDAY

Marks arrived at headquarters earlier than normal. He was up, dressed and raring to go this morning before 6am. He found it hard to understand how unpredictable Parkinson's could be. He hadn't had the best sleep, probably due to thinking about the Beaumont enquiry but he felt completely refreshed. Other days when he has had nearly ten hours sleep, he has felt exhausted when he got up.

He fired up his computer, retrieved his coffee cup from his top drawer, put a teaspoonful of decaf coffee in it and his usual, three sugars, and went to the kitchen to boil the kettle. He was in the kitchen when Sharpe came in. Marks offered to make him a coffee, an offer gladly taken up by Sharpe.

'Have you had the chance to log in yet?' said Sharpe.
'No, I fired up the computer then came in here to get a coffee,' replied Marks.

'I've been thinking. It must be the person he met up with on Thursday night that's done it. There's just too many coincidences for it not to be that person' said Sharpe.

'I agree. We'll see if there's been any development overnight and make a plan of action.'

'I presume you will be visiting Louise Beaumont today?'

'I imagine I will, but I'll see what's doing first, why is there something you want me to ask her?'

'Well I was thinking I'd tag along if that's ok with you?'

'Yes, that sound like a good idea. Like I said I'll see what's needing done, what new information there is, if any, and give Louise a phone to arrange a time.'

Marks thought it best to phone her to arrange a time first, but Sharpe thought it best they didn't phone because she would simply ask all her questions on the phone. This may prove difficult to avoid giving her all the information over the phone. If she isn't in, then they can phone her mobile and ask when she would be in.

Sharpe had convinced Marks that it may be best not to phone, but 'pop in' on the off chance to see if she's in.

Marks returned to his office coffee in hand. There had been very little crime, fortunately, throughout the night shift, which allowed Marks to read over the updated crime report of the body parts found in the bags. There was little difference to it from when he left yesterday but then again, he didn't think there would be because the locus is not overlooked by any houses. There's no cctv anywhere near the locus.

With so many cars coming and going to the park it would be very hard for anyone to appear out of the ordinary. But this didn't stop them issuing a press appeal, in the hope that somebody had seen something. However as the park is mainly used for football, although there is usually, a large number of dog walkers in the park, the lighting is extremely poor, so it's also highly unlikely that anyone would be able to identify anyone they thought was up to no good anyway.

Marks thought the only way they're going to catch this killer is through forensics picking up DNA from something. Although he was useless with technology, he thought they can probably find out who Beaumont planned on meeting through his social media accounts.

That would at least give them a starting point. Marks priority job for the morning was to contact their social media investigative officer who would hopefully provide them with the name of the person they thought he may have met.

Marks was thinking to himself how much times have changed since he was young. When he was young, he had friends who would give females a different surname so that they wouldn't realise his friends were dating more than one girl at a time. Nowadays people can virtually know everything about someone before they even have a date, if they research them on social media, there's no mystery left.

The problem, as far as Marks was aware, was that one person can create multiple accounts in different names. Marks figured Beaumont would have at least two, depending upon how many times he went undercover as someone different. Obviously one of the names they would check under would be Garry Flynn. But Marks felt he may have to contact Kelly again if they have no luck.

Before Marks could phone the social media officer, he received a phone call from the forensic lab. They had the results of the footwear comparisons of the footwear taken from the Liverpudlians in custody and the partial print found in Alan Starky's flat. They had a match. However it wasn't belonging to the footwear of Steven Fowler or Colin Crosby but to the footwear that belonged to Jon Paul Jackson.

Marks went to the incident room, where he found Sharpe and told him the news.

Crichton and Munro had finished the cctv review and they believe they've caught Fowler, Crosby and Jackson on cctv yards from the locus, walking towards it on the Friday evening at about quarter past six at night. The only downside to it, is that it's on a fixed camera from the homeless unit next door, which means we can't zoom in any further' said Sharpe.

'Brilliant' replied Marks before adding, 'all we need now is the murder weapon'

'Would be good if we can get that as well, but even if we don't the forensic evidence is enough to build a case against all three, and of course we still need to interview them so we may get something out of that' said Marks.

'Doubtful, but you never know'

'Yeah, they'll get lawyered up and give no comment interviews' said Sharpe.

(Lawyered up – simply means the suspect will speak to their lawyer who will tell them to say no comment to every question. While this is extremely frustrating for cops, everyone has the right to say nothing to any and every question asked by police)

'Still, that makes it three responsible for Stark's murder. Steven Fowler, Colin Crosby and Jon Paul Jackson and what made it even better is that all three are already in custody. Fowler and Jackson have been arrested on drugs charges whilst Crosby is being returned to prison for breaching conditions of his probation' said Marks.

'A good result' said Sharpe.

'Great result' said Marks as he continued 'it gets three violent men behind bars and there is no doubt that they would have committed more violent crime in the future.'

'Agreed. These types of guys don't change.'

Chapter 16

Marks contacted the social media officer and asked him to make it a priority to look at all the social media accounts for Barry Beaumont and Garry Flynn. Under the circumstances he said he would investigate it as soon as he could.

Marks was informed however that one person can make multiple accounts, on multiple forums, (Facebook, Twitter, Snapchat etc) and as far as the social media officer was aware of there is no way of him being able to verify they are all from the same person. Unless they all came from the same IP address (this address is unique to each internet connected device). Then again if it relates to a computer in a house that five people share, then the account could belong to any one of them. If all the accounts came from the same email address – then all the accounts could belong to the same person. Other than that the only other way of tying all the accounts to one person is if he went into each individual account and looked at photos uploaded by the person.

But even then, someone who is technically proficient can alter their IP address by various means. The same person may have different email accounts too. Unfortunately, this all meant that it may prove difficult to find all accounts on any forum for Barry Beaumont or the killer or killers.

The same thing applies for anyone joining dating websites. If they have separate emails, they can open various accounts.

This all sounded very technical to Marks, who, if he was being honest with himself, barely managed to understand what the social media officer was saying. However, he updated Sharpe and left it in the capable hands of the force expert.

In the meantime, Sharpe and Marks were going to visit Louise Beaumont. Marks didn't have a great deal more information to tell Louise, but he thought it would let her know that the police were there to support her. As they drove into Beaumont's street, they saw Louise get out of her car and go into the house.

Sharpe and Marks were about to get out the car when Sharpe received a phone call from the social media officer who had some information for them.

Sharpe put the call on speakerphone in order to let Marks hear what was being said.

'I've researched all the popular social media platforms and found that Beaumont had two Facebook accounts in the names of Barry Beaumont and Gary Flynn. However there is very little activity on both accounts and certainly nothing to indicate he had planned to meet anyone. However, I also checked out the most popular dating sites and got a hit.'

'Brilliant. Was he meeting someone on Thursday night?'

'Yes, but it wasn't a woman. He had arranged to meet a guy.'

'A guy!' said Marks in disbelief.

'I never saw that one coming' said Sharpe.

'Me neither' said Marks.

'The thing is' ……said the social media officer 'he's been very active on this site. As far as I can ascertain he's met up with at least four men within the last year.'

'Do you have names and dates' asked Sharpe.

'Yeah, I figured you'd need that, so I've saved all that information onto a pen drive.'

'That's brilliant thanks' said Marks.

'Do you have details of the person he was meeting on Thursday?' asked Sharpe.

'Yes, but it's probably an alias.'

'Ok, well forward all you have to me and DCI Marks via email please.'

'Ok, no problem, oh there's just one more thing.'

'Yeah what's that?' asked Marks.

'Judging by what he has written in his profile. Beaumont was no stranger to partaking in gay orgies.'

'Ok' said Sharpe, while Marks' face told Sharpe this was something he found disgusting.

'Thanks for the help' said Sharpe.

'No problem, bye.'

Marks said to Sharpe, 'I'll bet Louise doesn't even know he's bisexual.'

'We'll soon see' said Sharpe.

They got out of the car. The noise of the car doors closing prompted Louise to appear at her living room window. She met Marks and Sharpe at the door.

'Afternoon Louise, how are you today?' asked Marks.

'I've had better days chief inspector' said Louise in a low tone of voice, giving the impression it was taking her a great deal of effort to speak to

Marks. Marks believed their relationship had been soured after yesterday's visit because she addressed him as Chief Inspector rather than Conor. She had never called him anything other than Conor before this.

'This is my colleague Detective Chief Inspector Calum Sharpe; he's leading the investigation into Barry's disappearance' said Marks.

'You'd better come in' said Louise reluctantly.

'Thanks' said both officers as they entered the house.

'Go into the first room on the right'

Marks and Sharpe did as they'd been instructed. They stood in the living room waiting on Louise to give them permission to sit down. Louise asked them to sit and as they did, she addressed Marks.

'Have you gained any further information about what happened?' Marks replied 'Nothing concrete but we're getting new information all the time. However, there are a few things we need to clarify. Would you mind if we ask you a few questions about Barry?'

'Sure, if you think it'll help?'

'Louise, we've reviewed the information we have and it's highly unlikely Barry's disappearance is connected to his undercover work.'

'What makes you so confident about that?'

'We can't go into specifics, but we don't think the gang he infiltrated could have harmed Barry due to the last time he was seen and the time they were arrested in connection with other matters. The enquiry we've carried out so far indicates he may have met up with someone on Thursday night. I don't suppose you know if he was due to meet anyone on Thursday night?'

'No sorry I don't. You need to help me here Chief Inspector. You now think Barry was killed by someone he met, on that night?'

'It's a theory we have knowing what we know' said Marks.

Louise never said anything she sat on the edge of the armchair waiting on Marks elaborating on what he'd said. However, he went on. Do you mind if I ask you some quite personal information about Barry and your relationship?'

'Like what?'

'Has Barry ever cheated on you?'

Louise sighed and diverted her gaze from Marks' eyes to her feet.

'Yes' she said almost ashamedly, but that was years ago, and he's never given me reason to think he's done that again.'

'Louise, when he cheated on you, was it with a man or a woman?' asked Marks, who knew the answer, but he wanted to hear it from Louise.

Marks and Sharpe could see, the suggestion it may have been a man Barry had an affair with took Louise by surprise.

'It was a woman' said Louise sharply, as if she'd been insulted.

'I apologise if I offended you by asking if it may have been a man, he had an affair with, but we really need to know if you know if Barry was attracted to men?' asked Marks.

'Louise shook her head, sighed and sat right back in her chair.'

'Louise…' said Marks who knew by her body language that she knew he liked men but was embarrassed, probably even humiliated, before he was cut off by Louise.

'Yes I knew.'

'How long have you known' Marks asked.

'About 6 months. My laptop broke and I urgently needed to finish some work, so I borrowed Barry's laptop. He was away working apparently, and I somehow guessed his password. When I went on it, I noticed he had looked up some gay dating websites on his internet history. So I went into one and he had a photo of him and another guy kissing. It made me sick.'

'Did you confront him when he came home?' asked Marks.

'No I never let on. When he was a way out, I would look on the computer again to see if it were a one off. If it was, then I probably could've lived with that, but it wasn't. Every time he said he had to stay away he was with another man.'

'Why didn't you confront him?' asked Marks.

'I don't know. I guess I wanted it to pretend it wasn't happening.'

'How did it make you feel?' asked Marks.

'How do you think I felt?' said Louise.

Marks and Sharpe could see the hurt in her face.

Louise continued 'I felt humiliated. Here was me sitting in the house worried about my brave husband, out all hours, pretending to be in it for the good, fighting to make this world a better place and all this time, he was sleeping around with men!'

'So what did you do then?'

'I never did anything; I was weighing up my options when he said he had to go and stay away last weekend.'

'and had you decided what you were going to do?'

Marks and Sharpe could see Louise wasn't comfortable with these questions, but whether it was because they were too personal, or she had something else to hide they weren't sure for now.

'No, we've been together a long time, and I know it was about six months ago I discovered my husband was bisexual, but I still didn't understand how he could be like that and how I didn't know.'

'Do you think Barry knew you knew about his secret?'

'I don't know, I guess he could have but I don't think so.'

'Have you ever had an affair?' asked Marks.

Louise became very defensive, 'I don't see what relevance that has on your enquiry.'

Sharpe took the opportunity to step in here because he thought it may allow Louise to see him as the friendly cop.

'Louise, we're not here to upset you and I apologise if some of these questions are personal but we need to know as much information about your relationship in order to make more effective decisions to help trace Barry safe and well.'

'Look, you know as well as I do that Barry isn't coming back. His bank cards were found in a bag that contained body parts. How could you explain that without it being his body parts in the bag?' asked Louise.

'Well...' before Marks or Sharpe could offer up a reason, Louise interrupted

'You can't. Look I appreciate you coming around and keeping me up to date with the latest information but I'd rather you leave me to come to grips with the fact my husband is missing, presumed murdered.'

'Louise, I'm not going to lie, it's possible that your right but until we have conclusive proof to confirm that we need to live in hope' said Marks.

'Louise, is there any reason that Barry would go missing? Is there any chance, regardless how slim it may be?'

'No at least not that I can think of.'

'Why are you so sure?'

'We've been married for 15 years, I think I know my husband, well I suppose I thought I did until six months ago. No reason he'd go missing. He has a good job; I have a good job we don't want for anything. I really can't see it.'

'Ok' said Marks.

'We'll go and continue our investigations; we'll be in touch.'
They all got up and Sharpe opened the doors for them. As they were leaving Marks said 'Thanks for your time Louise. If you need to talk about anything, give me a call anytime.'

'Thanks' she said with a little smile.

Sharpe started the car and off they went, to return to headquarters where they would continue the hunt for Barry Beaumont. Sharpe and Marks discussed what Louise had said during their visit. They both formed the opinion that Louise had been unfaithful at some point in the past, due to her body language and her attempts to avoid the question. But they both believed she was mourning the loss of her husband.

Chapter 17

TUESDAY

Sharpe had made the coffees for both him and Marks which allowed Marks the extra couple of minutes to open and start reading the file he had been sent by the force's Social Media Officer.
Marks didn't recognise the Barry Beaumont he knew on the images. The one he knew was a devoted husband who dressed smartly and was an introvert. The Barry Beaumont in these images was one who appeared to be very promiscuous, outgoing and a sado-masochist. There were numerous photos indicating that he liked to be physically hurt in order to enjoy his encounters. It was two different people. Marks wondered how long he had lived this life. It certainly seemed like he was happy within himself and comfortable in his surroundings. It didn't strike Marks as someone who had recently discovered their liking for this kind of life.

There were lots of images of him with various men and in various poses with these men. When he saw some of the photos and read some of the posts made by Beaumont, he understood why Louise Beaumont had felt humiliated, hurt and angry.

Fortunately the social media officer had detailed all the times and dates of men he had arranged to meet on gay web sites, albeit, these were the only ones they knew he was connected to, there may have been more under different names.

Marks wondered how many of these men had wives too.

The important one was the last entry. He had planned to meet someone called BIGBRIAN8. However, they didn't have a great deal more information on him, at least from this site. There were plenty of photographs, but in most of them the people were wearing masks. The pictures that showed the faces could've been of anyone because they had nothing to compare it to. What they needed was a check with the driving licence authority to compare it to the driving licence photo or an image on the police systems of the male if there was one. But before they could do any of this, they would need to find out his full name and date of birth, but at least they had a place to start.

9pm at Relax bar in Dundee on Friday was the time Beaumont was to meet big Brian. They would hopefully have cctv that covered the entrance/exit to the premises which would hopefully catch the two together. DC Masters had been tasked with contacting the manager of Relax in order to secure the footage.
Masters contacted the manager and they agreed he would go round to the bar at 3pm and the manager would make sure the footage was ready to be viewed. Masters thanked him for accommodating the request so quickly and said he would see him at 3pm.

Ricky Simpson was an experienced plumber. He'd been a plumber for over ten years and had recently began working for himself. The hours were long, but the rewards made it worthwhile. It allowed him to spend every weekend with his daughter Tiffany, who stayed with his ex-wife and treat her to whatever she wanted, whether that was money to go out with friends or spend time at the ice rink with her dad.

He was in the process of trying to recruit another plumber such was the volume of work. He already had a three-week backlog of work, which he appreciated sounded great but at the same time he knew if it was going to take that long to fix someone's problem, they'd end up going elsewhere.

The first job of today was to a house where the resident was complaining that their drains appeared blocked. Ricky went to the house and spoke to the resident Mr Wheeler whose drains appeared blocked. Wheeler was an older gentleman who was hard of hearing. He had two hearing aids but seldom remembered to replace the old batteries. He offered Ricky a cup of tea or coffee but being the first job of the day Ricky declined the offer. He did however tell Mr Wheeler to fill the kettle in the meantime because he would need to switch the water off. Mr Wheeler said he would fill the kettle so if he changed his mind just to give him a shout because he'd be in the living room.

Ricky went to work. After a while he discovered what the problem was, it was a blocked pipe. Ricky could see a lump of white sludge was causing the blockage. It took Ricky sometime to dislodge the sludge, but when he did, he looked at it and kept looking at it until it dawned on him what he was looking at, it was part of a forearm. He was shocked and scared in equal measure because it appeared to him to be human flesh in the drain. Could the man he was speaking to an hour ago be a killer? Surely not, he must be about seventy years old, thought Ricky.

His mind started racing, he had to tell the police, but what if the resident hears him? If he's killed somebody before there's nothing to say he won't kill me. Ricky took several deep breaths and composed himself.

'Mr Wheeler, I've got to go and get a new pipe for the toilet. I'll be back as soon as I can, probably be about half an hour.'
'Ok. I'll leave the door unlocked so just knock and come in.' said Wheeler.
'Ok, no problem' said Ricky.

Ricky drove to the nearest police station which was police headquarters where he literally grabbed the first person he saw coming out of headquarters.

'Are you a police officer?'
'Yes, can I help you, are you alright' said DS Bailey. She could see Ricky was pure white and in a panicked state.

'I went to a house today because there was apparently a blockage in the system. When I found the blockage it was piece of human flesh' said Ricky who by now was becoming more nervous as the dawn realisation of what he'd witnessed was beginning to hit home.

'Come with me' said Bailey as she took him by the arm and led him into the building.
'you're pure white, are you feeling faint?'
'No, I just need a seat and I'll be fine' said Ricky.

Bailey took him into the first free interview room she found. 'Wait here I'll be back in a minute.'
She phoned the incident room; the phone was picked up by DC Whyte. She told him to tell DCI Sharpe to come down to the interview room beside the PEO (Public enquiry office) ASAP.
She returned to the room where Ricky told her what he'd found.

A few minutes later Sharpe knocked on the door and popped his head in to make sure it was the right room they were in.

He entered the room and Bailey updated him with what she'd been told by Ricky. Sharpe asked Bailey to get a proper statement whilst he went into the CID office and instructed all the detectives to attend at the incident room now. He knocked on Marks' door before opening it and asking Marks to attend at the incident room now.

When everyone had gathered there, he told them the reason why he'd called everyone in.
The need to preserve evidence and secure Mr Wheeler, who will be treated as a witness at this time.
'Why isn't he being treated as a suspect?' asked one of the detectives.

Sharpe replied 'before he's a suspect we need to establish a crime has been committed. Now it's just a piece of sludge, we will need to recover the sludge and analyse it, if it transpires that it is human flesh then we'll deal with that accordingly.'

Sharpe tasked DS Bailey with applying for an evidential search warrant. In the meantime Sharpe and several officers were going to attend the home address of Mr Wheeler and ask him to accompany them to headquarters.

Meanwhile, DC Sharma was tasked with researching all the information she could find on the address and on all the occupants they knew had lived there, including Mr Wheeler. It could have been a lengthy task but actually turned out to be a relatively short one because according to the police systems, Mr George Wheeler was the only person linked to that address and that was as someone who had phoned police about suspected bogus workmen.

Sharpe and several detectives along with two uniform officers attended at Wheelers home address. Sharpe had been shown mages of men in the hope that he would recognise the male who called himself Big Brian, as the occupant of the house.

Bailey hammered on the door and a few seconds later heard inaudible shouts coming from inside. As Bailey began to knock again, they heard someone making their way to the door. The door opened and there stood an elderly gentleman with thick specs, two hearing aids, and a walking stick. This clearly wasn't the man they were looking for.

Bailey informed the man who they were and asked the gentleman who he was 'George Wheeler' came the reply. Bailey identified herself and her colleagues as Police Officers and asked Mr Wheeler if they could come in to talk to him. Without any hesitation he said ok and turned around to walk back to where he'd came. Bailey, Sharpe and the detectives all walked in, following the shuffling man into his living room.

He sat down and turned the tv off, which was just well thought Sharpe because it would've been impossible to talk over. Mr Wheeler looked around at the squad of police now standing in his house.

'What can I do for you officers?' said Mr Wheeler.
'Mr Wheeler, I'm Detective Chief Inspector Sharpe, do you live here on your own?'
'You'll need to speak up son, I'm deaf.'

Sharpe repeated what he had said to the point where he was almost shouting.

'No. My son Brian lives here with me. He moved in about three years ago when his mum died.'

'Where is he now?'

'He's at work.'

'What time will he be in?'

'I think he said he was finishing at five, so he'll be in about half five - quarter to six.'

'Mr Wheeler we're here because the plumber found something in the pipes that looked like human flesh.'

'Human flesh. Agh, he must be on that 'Waccy Baccy' all them young anes are on that now.
Human flesh, it's probably a rat or something. He must be stoned, bloody hippy.'

Mr Wheeler may have been slow to get round, but he certainly wasn't slow up top.

Sharpe went on 'Mr Wheeler, could you come with us down to police headquarters for a chat.'

'Just ask me what you want to ask here detective.'

'I'd prefer it if you come down to the police station with us' said Sharpe.

'Who's going to bring me back?' asked Mr Wheeler.

'Don't worry we'll sort something out' said Sharpe.

'Mr Wheeler do you mind if we have a look around the house?'

'No go ahead I've nothing to hide.'

'That's great, thanks for that Mr Wheeler. Do you need any medication with you?'

'No. I'll be fine son.'

'Do you want to be here whilst some of my officers search the house?'

'No. There's nothing to find anyway.'

Sharpe however, still had DS Budd apply for the evidential search warrant, after all Mr Wheeler can change his mind at any point. Although the most likely scenario is that his son, (who's the person Sharpe believed they were now looking for) would ask them to stop searching. They would then have to apply for a warrant. At least if they had the warrant, if permission to search has been revoked then they have the warrant at hand.

Sharpe paired up the officers and asked them to carry out a cursory search of the property which they did. They found that the main bedroom upstairs was locked, and that the entire upstairs had been thoroughly cleaned. Downstairs was tidy but it wasn't as clean as the upstairs rooms had been. Mr Wheeler couldn't manage the stairs these days and so lived downstairs. There was a bathroom downstairs to accommodate Mr Wheeler.

Sharpe wasn't concerned by the fact the bedroom was locked because they would force it open when they obtained the evidential warrant.

He had also been informed that there was a shed which was secured by an extremely large padlock that they would need to search. When Mr Wheeler was asked about his pipes appearing to be blocked, he made an innocent comment which may end up being crucial to the police's investigation. He said he's had trouble with his pipes for the last couple of years. They were apparently always getting blocked. But he didn't worry because his son Brian always took care of it. He just thought he would give him a break and get a plumber in to do it for him.

Sharpe asked DC Crichton to take the witness statement from Mr Wheeler, whilst he told Munro to start arranging a search team to search the property. This search would require at least four searchers and a POLSA (Police Search Adviser) to detail who was searching each room and whether they found anything and if they did where exactly it was found.

During this witness statement Crichton asked some questions to clarify a few points including his son's sexuality. Wheeler replied that his son was gay, but that he was in a relationship. He said Brian was going to be introducing him to the boyfriend soon but hadn't done so yet. Crichton asked him if Brian had told him the name of his boyfriend but Mr Wheeler said he thought he had but he couldn't remember what it was. When asked if Brian had brought men home before Mr Wheeler said no, but also said he can be quite forgetful. Crichton stopped taking a statement at this point because it was becoming apparent that Mr Wheeler was getting confused at times and she didn't think that it was in Mr Wheelers best interests to continue.

She read the statement over to Mr Wheeler to ensure the content of his statement was a true reflection on what he'd said. He agreed it was and signed the statement. Crichton made sure she had Mr Wheelers comment about having bother with the pipes since his son moved in was recorded, as well as a few other valuable pieces of information. However, she was now of the opinion that Mr Wheeler couldn't be classed as a credible witness due to his forgetfulness which she suspected was probably the early stages of Alhzeimers or dementia.

She offered Mr Wheeler a cup of tea or coffee which he gladly accepted. Crichton brought Mr Wheeler his tea and a small plate of biscuits through from the kitchen. She told him to help himself and that she'd be back in a few minutes.

Mr Wheeler asked Crichton if he could home now. Crichton asked him if there was anywhere else they could stay for the night, if there were any other family members they could stay with. Mr Wheeler said there wasn't. Crichton contacted Sharpe to tell him what Mr Wheeler had said but that she didn't think he could be classed as a credible witness due to his forgetfulness. Sharpe agreed and said that if they ended up detaining his son then they would be required to contact social work to have Mr Wheeler looked after in the interim. His long term needs would have to be discussed with other partner agencies but it was beginning to look like he would need to be placed in a care home.

She returned to the CID office where the searchers, who had all turned up now, were waiting to be briefed. She spoke briefly to Sharpe and Bailey. Sharpe however did say he'd come along and speak to Mr Wheeler after the briefing.

As Sharpe was beginning his briefing, he was interrupted by the control room on the radio, who were informing him that Brian Wheeler had returned home and wasn't happy that he was not allowed in his home.

Sharpe told Bailey and DC Davie to go to the house straight away and get Brian Wheeler down to headquarters as soon as possible.

He returned to the briefing where he informed the POLSA and search teams what was required of them and DC Mason who would be attending in his role as videographer/photographer, not that Mason needed a briefing he was one of the most experienced SOCO's in the force. Sharpe then went along to speak to Mr Wheeler.

He was on his way to speak to Mr Wheeler when yet again he was stopped in his tracks. This time by Marks, who had an important update for him. Wright had popped in to see Marks after he'd taken Mr Wheelers statement as instructed by Marks. When he spoke to Mr Wheeler, he obtained the full name and date of birth for his son. Marks then checked with the DVLA, who were very helpful and sent up a copy of his driving licence, which had a photo of Brian Wheeler on it.

Marks compared this photo with some of the photos they had obtained from the gay website. Marks found that Brian Wheeler was in some photos with Barry Beaumont in various poses, and that some of the photos of them both had been taken as long as 3 months ago.

Marks and Sharpe both agreed that to them it looked like Marks and Wheeler were involved in a relationship. But if this were the case, they couldn't explain why they had planned to meet on this website. Still that's a question for later, for now they would concentrate on gathering evidence.

Sharpe finally got round to speaking to Mr Wheeler. He said that if they are not finished by 9pm then the force would pay for him and his son to stay elsewhere for the night. Mr Wheeler couldn't understand why they wouldn't be finished by that time. Sharpe took a bit of time to explain to him the reasons why it may take time and he appeared to understand. He also explained that if this were the case then they would allow him to return home to pick up anything he needed for the night.
In the meantime he could go to the force's canteen, where they would get him something to eat and drink. They would also put the telly on for him.

This however meant someone would be tasked with staying with him whilst he was there.

Bailey phoned Sharpe. Brian Wheeler was refusing to go anywhere. He was extremely angry at police for taking his elderly father down to headquarters without his (Brian's) consent. Bailey informed him however, that they believed that when they asked his father to come down to headquarters that he was fully aware of what was being asked, therefore they did not need his consent to take his father to headquarters. However, they had to accept that their initial belief that his father was able to comprehend what was being asked was probably incorrect. Bailey asked Mr Wheeler if there was anyone else his father could stay with for the night if the search would result in him being taken to police headquarters but he said he was the only family his father had. Brian Wheeler asked what would happen to his father if he couldn't return home somehow. When he asked this Bailey immediately thought we are definitely going to find something incriminating here otherwise he wouldn't have asked that question. She explained that if that's the case then the police would ensure his father is placed in a care home temporarily until a permanent solution could be found.

Brian Wheeler calmed down, after his initial bout of anger, once he was told what may happen to his father if he was to be detained or arrested. But he still refused to go to headquarters. Bailey thought that Brian Wheeler appeared to have accepted what was going to happen to him, it was as if he knew the game was up, which was why she thought he had calmed down. At this point she fully expected her search team colleagues to find some incriminating evidence.

The searchers planned to carry out the search systematically but upon speaking to Bailey they decided to start in the bathroom where the plumber had found the white sludge. They found the white sludge the plumber had discovered, and they knew it was human flesh. It also had the smell of rotten flesh. However, they weren't medically trained to provide their opinion, so they bagged it and labelled it to be sent for analysis. Despite the time (it had now gone 7pm) Dr Dempster the force pathologist stayed in the mortuary waiting for the white sludge in order to give Sharpe an answer asap. This would allow them to begin preparing an interview for Brian Wheeler.

Although they had researched the property and had the names of the previous tenants, they hadn't stayed there for almost 20 years, so the person who flushed this white sludge down the toilet must have been someone who had stayed at the house recently. By George Wheeler's own admission, only himself and his son have stayed there since Brian moved in almost three years ago.

The search team also found more pieces of white sludge in the piping.

Brian Wheeler had gone very quiet in the last ten to fifteen minutes which Bailey thought was strange considering how vocal he'd been beforehand.

'Brian, why is the upstairs bedroom locked?' asked Bailey.
He replied, 'so that if my dad doesn't go into it just in case, he does make it upstairs.'
'Why is there something there that you wouldn't want him to see?' asked Bailey.
'Yes. I may as well tell you; you're going to find them anyway.'
'What are we going to find?'
'The body parts wrapped in polythene under the bed and there's something in the wardrobe too.'

Bailey's reaction was one of shock, which Brian clearly saw in her face. He said, 'look in the wardrobe there's a surprise for you,' as he smiled at Bailey.

Bailey cautioned him and reminded him that he doesn't need to say anything at all, but she hoped he would continue talking. What prompted her to ask that question, she wasn't sure, probably because they were hanging around waiting on the search team finishing and she had been on since 7am and she was hungry and getting tired.

Bailey asked, 'where's the key for the bedroom?'

'Here' said Brian as he took the key from his keyring and handed it to her. He then said 'you'd better take this one as well' and handed Bailey a key for a padlock.

'What's this for?' asked Bailey.

'The garden shed. That's where I cut up the bodies, there's body parts in there too' replied Brian Wheeler.

Bailey looked at him in disbelief, not just because there were bodies (plural) in the shed but at the indifferent attitude shown by Brian Wheeler. He said it like it was a normal occurrence.

Bailey shouted on DC Anderson, who was the POLSA and she gave him the key. She told him what Brian Wheeler had just said and he went straight back upstairs and opened the bedroom door. Straight away he looked under the bed and sure enough there were two rolls off polythene with something
inside each roll. Anderson looked at Mason who was already filming this.

Anderson pulled the polythene parcels out from under the bed. He unravelled the first one and as he carefully pulled back the last bit of polythene covering the item, they saw it was a human head, with the eyes missing and a human torso. Anderson did the same with the next polythene parcel, this time it was four arms minus the hands. Just when Anderson didn't think it could get any worse, he opened the wardrobe and found a large glass jar with a number of eyeballs in liquid.

There sitting on a shelf was a dinner plate with head on it. The eyeballs were still in the head.

Even for seasoned searchers who had searched numerous crime scenes and found various body parts in various stages of decomposition, this was gruesome, and they hadn't even opened the shed yet. God only knows what lay in store for them there.

Anderson went downstairs and spoke to Bailey. She was in still in disbelief at Brian's earlier comment. Bailey phoned Sharpe straight away. He would attend the house very shortly to see for himself.

When Sharpe arrived, he spoke to Bailey before going to the bedroom to see what had been found. He looked in the wardrobe and saw the eyeballs in the jar. He immediately recognised the head was Barry Beaumont. However, they would need to identify the other victim or victims.

Bailey and Sharpe then went outside into the rear garden where sitting at the end of a well maintained garden was a large shed. There were no windows and the shed was secured by a large padlock. Sharpe unlocked the door and looked at Bailey. She looked at him with a hint of dread in her eyes. Sharpe opened the door and was hit by the stench of death. He felt around for a light switch, finding one just inside the door. The lights came on and shone on the scene that few people would have ever imagined sat in the shed of a seemingly harmless local bus driver. There was a home-made table, approximately seven or eight foot long, with straps for the arms and legs. The table was soaked in blood. On the back wall everything had it's place. Hung on nails, there was a variety of saws, hacksaws, hammers, meat cleavers, rope and a leather apron. Below this was a table with a kettle, cup, spoons and a Tupperware box with some biscuits inside.

Placed up against one of the other walls, was an old large bookcase which had a number of skulls on the top shelf, on the others were various body parts. Once Sharpe and Bailey managed to take in just what they were seeing, they noticed that the shed had been soundproofed.

Bailey and Davie detained Brian Wheeler and took him to headquarters.

Whilst they were en route to headquarters Sharpe called Davie and told him to tell Bailey that Dr Dempster had been on the phone. She was able to confirm that the white sludge was in fact part of a human arm. Bailey thought on any other day this would be a strange thing to hear but today…..no. As far as bad days at the office go, this was by far the worst day you could have.

Meanwhile, Sharpe updated Marks, who by this time (it was now 830pm) was at home. Sharpe said he wanted Marks to know but that he was aware he'd be home, and he wasn't expecting him to do anything.

Marks told Sharpe that under the circumstances he would return to work. But only to inform Louise Beaumont, it's the least she deserves. Sharpe told him what had happened in the last few hours and what was going to happen now. Marks said he would go straight to Louise's house and inform her of the latest developments.

Chapter 18

2115 hours, and Marks pulled up outside Louise Beaumont's house. There were two cars in the drive, this must mean Louise has company. Marks rang the doorbell and knocked on the door. Louise approached the door and looked out a side window panel to see who it was and on seeing Marks she opened the door.

'Come in Conor. Just go through to the living room' said Louise. Marks was being greeted by a welcoming Louise Beaumont which wasn't exactly what he was expecting. Marks sat down then waited on Louise sitting down before he broke the news.

'Louise, I'm very sorry to have to tell you this but Barry's dead. We've found his body in a house. I'm really sorry Louise.'
'To be honest Conor, I was expecting that,' she said rather bluntly. 'I knew the last time you were here with your colleague DCI Sharpe that it was just a matter of time before you found him. You said you found him in a house. Whose house is it?'

Marks thought Louise appeared very matter of fact about what she'd been told. Marks had passed many death messages in his time and although everyone reacts differently, he thought Louise was indifferent to the news. Then again, she is a very clever person and probably knew the chances of finding Barry alive were very slim, especially after his personal cards were found in bags containing body parts.

'It's the house of a man he was dating apparently. He's been detained now, and we'll be interviewing him tonight.'
'What's his name?'.
'What difference will it make, knowing his name?'

'Probably none but I'd like to know who's responsible for my husband's death.'

'He's only a suspect now.'

'Conor. You know I'm a lawyer. You know I've defended people like this before. You know and I know if the body of a victim is found in a house then it will be someone from that household who's responsible for that death. Even if you tell me, I won't say to anyone, I'd just like to know.'

'I guess there's no harm in telling you, after all you may have relevant information regarding this male and Barry's relationship. Louise does the name Brian Wheeler mean anything to you. Has Barry ever mentioned a male by that name?'

'Relationship? How long had this been ongoing for?'

'From what we can tell, we think about 3 months'

'Three months!'' shouted Louise who was obviously very angry at this.

'Did you have any idea he was having an affair?

'No, I mean I'm not saying it's coming as a total shock. He's had an affair before and the gay websites he was looking up were eye opening for me, but I thought he was happy, some lawyer I am not even catching on her husband is having an affair with a man.'

'How could you know? Barry said he was working. You believed him and I think a lot of people would. Did he ever mention Brian Wheeler to you?'

'Not that I can recall.'

'Is Barry's laptop here?'

'I don't think so, but I'll have a look for it in the morning and I'll bring it to headquarters if I find it, if that's ok?

'That's fine. Is there anyone you'd like me to inform about Barry, his parents or his brother,' said Marks.

'No, it's ok. I'll phone his brother and he can let his parents know' said Louise.

Marks was aware it would have looked incredibly insensitive for him to insist she looks for Barry's laptop now. Tomorrow would be fine. Marks asked her if there was anything, she needed to know from him, but she said no, but that she still had his phone number from a previous visit, should she need to speak to him. Marks told her to phone anytime and said he'd go for now. Louise thanked him for coming and saw Marks out before locking the door.

Marks looked up at the bedroom and caught someone peeking out behind a curtain. He thought it looked like a male, but he couldn't be sure, he just caught a glimpse of the person as they closed the curtains. He did see that they had a cast on their left arm. Louise had company. She never said she had someone in but then again it was no business of Marks' if she had someone else in the house.

Marks was going to take note of the licence plate of the car but thought, even if it is a boyfriend's car, so what, she has done nothing illegal. He could check who the car belonged to, and who it was insured for, but he had no justifiable reason to do that. Although her husband had been found dead, he'd had several affairs it seems throughout their married life, so why should it be different for her.

Brian Wheeler had been fully researched on all police systems prior to him being taken to police headquarters. This was certainly going to be a new experience for him because he had never been in any bother with the police before.

He wouldn't spend long in a police cell before he was interviewed probably two hours at most. Sharpe's thinking was that Wheeler was quite forthcoming with information and he wanted that to continue

Chapter 19

TUESDAY /WEDNESDAY

Sharpe was an experienced interviewer, but he was going to allow DS Lisa Bailey to lead the interview. Their plan was to ask a few simple open-ended questions to Wheeler and let him talk. The only problem with this would be if his lawyer told him to say no comment and Wheeler took this advice.

The interview would be recorded on dvd and on cd. Bailey read out the time, date, who was present, and why they were there. By now it was 11pm.

The following is excerpts from the interview.

Bailey: Mr Wheeler, we obtained an evidential search warrant for your home address, at 11 Glenville Avenue, Dundee which we executed today. During this search we found seven human heads, the torso of a white male, the arms of two white males, six pairs of hands and a jar with eighteen eyeballs. What can you tell me about this?

Wheeler: The head that has the eyes still in them is Garry Flynn although I think his right name is Barry Beaumont. But then again Garry might be his real name I'm not sure. I can't recall the names of the other people's skulls or body parts.

Bailey: Are all the body parts we've found in your house and shed, body parts of people you killed?

Wheeler: Yeah.

Bailey: How many people have you killed?

Wheeler: I'm not sure nine, ten maybe. I don't know.

Bailey: When did you murder your first victim?

Wheeler: Three years ago.

Bailey: Are you telling me that you have murdered nine or ten people in three years?

Wheeler: Yeah. (Who didn't seem at all fussed about it)

Bailey: Getting back to Barry Beaumont. How did you know Mr Beaumont?

Wheeler: He was my partner for three months.

Bailey: How did you meet?

Wheeler: We met through a gay website. At first it was just sexual, then we started a relationship. But then he wouldn't leave his wife for me. He wanted to stay with her and have me as his bit on the side. But I told him, time and time again I wasn't going to tolerate it. He had to choose, me or her.

Bailey: Then what happened?

Wheeler: We were in the kitchen, it was Friday morning and I was making him breakfast, when yet again we argued about him not leaving his wife. I got really pissed off because he said he wouldn't leave her and that he wished he'd never met me. After everything I did for him! I wasn't going to let him treat me like that so I stabbed him a load of times. He was on the floor groaning, and I was kneeling on him. I kissed his forehead then stabbed him a couple of more times until he shut up. There was blood everywhere. I was still a bit angry at what he said so I took him straight to the shed where I cut him up. But talk about having no luck. I could only find three black bags, so I put some of him in each of the bags. But I didn't want them to be too heavy coz then people might notice me struggling with the bags and then they might ask questions. So I put the bags out in the car, once I put some polythene down, so the blood wouldn't seep into the car.

Then I wrapped his arms in one piece of polythene and put his head on a plate and put it in the wardrobe. The rest of him was in bags.
Bailey: And this was last Friday?
Wheeler: Yeah
Bailey: Wasn't your father in the house?
Wheeler: Yes, but he's almost deaf and if I make his meals he won't go in the kitchen.
Bailey: What did you use to cut him up?
Wheeler: I used an electric saw, because I've found it takes ages with a hacksaw and a meat cleaver. It's a lot quicker with an electric saw. That reduces the time it takes to cut up a body quite substantially. It's not easy cutting up a dead body you know. The first time I did it I was sweating because it took me ages.

Bailey and Sharpe looked at each other in disbelief at Wheeler's comments.

Bailey: What made you start to kill, I mean you were in your forties when you started, why then?
Wheeler: The first one was accidental. I met a guy through a website, and we went back to mine. We were having sex and he asked me to strangle him when he was nearly there, but I went too far and killed him. I was scared, but I found it strangely exhilarating. I cut up his body so that I could dispose of it more easily. I chucked the body parts in black bin bags and put them in bins that were out on the street, because I thought they must be out for pick up. I kept waiting on the police coming to my door but when they never came, I got quite excited by the thrill of it and I had to do it again.
Bailey: Do you remember the male's name?
Wheeler: No, Barry or Garry, whatever his real name was, is the only name I can remember. They were all guys I met through online sex sites and nobody puts their real names on there.

At this point, there was a knock on the door. This was a sign that someone had something urgent to speak to Sharpe and Bailey about.

Bailey stopped the interview and Sharpe left the room momentarily. When he returned, he passed a note to Bailey? The note read; Search team found a book detailing, who Wheeler met up with, when they met, where they went, what they did, how he murdered them. All dated and timed.

When Bailey informed Wheeler what they had found, his lawyer immediately told him to say no comment and expressed his desire to have a private conversation with his client.

Sharpe and Bailey allowed them to have a discussion. Afterwards, Wheeler refused to answer any more questions.
Sharpe and Bailey concluded the interview a few hours later and charged him with the murder of Barry Beaumont. There would of course be further charges to prefer against Wheeler once the identity of victims had been established and dates the murders occurred between.

Chapter 20

The following day Marks contacted Louise to tell her that Brian Wheeler had been arrested, cautioned and charged with her husband's murder. She thanked him for the update and said she was about to call him to let him know she had Barry's laptop and that she would hand it in to headquarters later.

Whilst Brian Wheeler was being interviewed the search team found a journal hidden under the floorboards of his bedroom. The journal had details of times and dates of all his killings in which Wheeler even stated how he killed his victim. They had found that he had apparently killed nine other people in the space of three years.

Marks suspected the reason they weren't aware off these victims is because Wheeler carefully selected them from gay web sites. He specifically targeted people from out of town and were single. Beaumont was the exception. The journal proved to police that Brian Wheeler knew exactly what he was doing before, during and after the murders of his victims.

As Sharpe reflected on his first big case in Dundee, he was pleased that everything went well from an operational sense. His team of detectives worked very well as a unit during an investigation that seemed like a hard slog at times, especially when it seemed like they were treading water, but their perseverance paid off.

He could count on Marks, at least for a little while, to back him up and to learn from, which also pleased him. Something told him he was going to enjoy working in this beautiful but crazy city.

It was late evening when Louise Beaumont was sitting in the conservatory thinking of all that had gone on when the phone rang. She didn't particularly feel like talking but when she looked at the phone, she saw it was from a number out with Britain. She didn't recognise the area code, so she answered it.

'Hello'
'Hello Louise?' asked the voice on the other end of the phone.
'Yes this is Louise. Who's this?'
'Don't say you've forgotten me already' asked the caller quizzingly.
'Your voice does sound familiar. Is that you Mr MacDonald?'
'No, that's disappointing I'd thought you would have recognised my voice Mrs Robinson' said the man obviously letting her know who was on the phone without giving his real name. Louise knew as soon as he said that who was on the phone.
'Ben (Braddock – from the film The Graduate). What are you doing contacting me?' said Louise.
'I heard about what happened to Barry. Sorry to hear that, I know that's probably a bit rich coming from me, especially considering what we got up to in his bed, but I never wished him any harm' said Ben.
'Thanks for that'.
'So who's Mr MacDonald, a boyfriend?'
'No, a business associate.'
'Ok. I believe you, others wouldn't but I will. How are you getting on?'
'I'm doing ok. I mean I'll miss him I guess, but the insurance money will help ease the pain' said Louise in a cold matter of fact way.
'Well, at least that's something. How much are you getting?'
'Over three hundred and fifty thousand'
'I take it you had a sizeable life insurance policy on him?' asked Ben.
'Oh yes. I mean he was working under cover and dealing with some serious villains. If they were to find out his real identity, then who knows what would've happened. So we increased his life insurance policy in case something happened.'

'So he knew about it?'

'Yes he knew. Barry was old fashioned that way. He wanted to make sure I would be alright if something happened to him'.

'How's your business doing?'

'Great I'm very busy now'

'That's good. How's your other business?'

'It'd died down just now, but it's always there. I take it there were no problems when you left?'

'No, it couldn't have gone any smoother'

'And how is life in Russia?'

'Good. I miss home but obviously I can't come home.'

'I know. How are you getting on learning the language?'

'It's getting easier now I know some of the locals.

'No regrets. I mean apart from getting in with that Psycho.'

'Plenty of regrets but at least I'm not in prison. An ex-cop in prison. I wouldn't last the week. You know I didn't willingly help Bell kill those women do you?'

'After the time we spent together, I think I know you well enough to say I know you wouldn't have willingly helped murder those women.'

'Thanks for that. I better get going. Take care.'

'Take care Ben' said Louise before ending the call.

Louise and Ben were clever. Although it had been a year since the serial killings took place in Dundee, police were still looking to capture Scott Young who had apparently helped Paul Bell commit those crimes.

Mrs Robinson (AKA Louise) didn't believe that Scott Young could be partly responsible for murdering three women. So when he reached out to her to help him escape the police she gladly provided him with the names of people who could provide a passport and safe passage to Russia. It may not have been the Bahamas but at least it was a non-extradition country and he wouldn't have to be constantly watching his back.

However, they still took precautions. They didn't use their right names on the call. Louise's judgement could be questioned at that time, because she and Young were having an affair when he became a suspect in the case. But because she didn't think he was willingly involved she assisted him in escaping to Russia.

She thought about what Marks had said that Barry had been dismembered. She hoped he had been killed before this had happened. She couldn't lie to herself. She didn't love Barry and hadn't been in love with him for some time but she didn't want him to suffer. She stayed with him because she thought they could work at it and things would work out fine. The truth of the matter, however, was that deep down, she knew they wouldn't be able to save their marriage.

The writing was on the wall years ago when Barry had a one-night stand with a female colleague. But Louise forgave him because she loved him, and he promised it was a one off. They had worked hard at their marriage afterwards but even she was shocked to find Barry had used gay websites to meet men within the last year. She felt humiliated but afterwards relieved because this gave her a reason to begin divorce proceedings, which she was in the process of doing. She also used that to justify having affairs.

She'd had a passionate affair with Scott Young but that had to end when he was being sought after by the police for his part in murdering three women. Louise didn't believe he could be involved in something like this which is why she helped him escape to Russia.

However, soon after that she bumped into Robbie whilst they were both out for the night approximately two months ago. Despite her failing marriage and Robbie being in a relationship they couldn't hide their feelings for one another and began having an affair.

Robbie soon split with his girlfriend as his and Louise's affair continued even after they were almost caught one night when Barry appeared home earlier than anticipated causing Robbie to hide in her side of the wardrobe until Barry fell asleep. An incident like this might have cooled other people from having an affair, but not Robbie and Louise. They were besotted with each other and even Louise couldn't believe how little it bothered her that Barry was gone, because it opened up the way for her and Robbie to have an open relationship.

She phoned Robbie.

'Robbie hi it's Louise.'

'Hi Louise, how's life?'

'Robbie, I'm sorry I don't know how to tell you this, but Barry's been murdered.'

'Murdered. What do you mean murdered, he's in the police, police officers don't get murdered?'

'Sorry Robbie, but he's been murdered.'

'How?' asked a puzzled Robbie.

'The police found parts of his body in bags beside a bin at football pitches. Then a few days later they traced a male Barry had been having sex with. When they went to this guy's house, they found the rest of Barry's body.'

'Fucking hell, this will kill mum.'

'I'm sorry Robbie, is there anything I can do?' asked a concerned Louise.

'No, I'll just need some time to sort things out.'

'Ok. I don't want to sound insensitive, but when will I see you again?'

'Louise, my brother's been murdered and you want to know when you'll see me next?'

'Yeah, well let's be honest, I'm not gonna miss Barry and now that he's out of the picture we can be together.'

'I won't miss him much either. I mean he was maybe a dick at times but he didn't deserve that. I'll be round once I make sure my mum's ok. Might be a good few days, but don't worry, I'll give you phone.'

'Ok.'

'Take care.'

THE END